He was attracted to her. Even when they'd been just friends.

But he knew himself well enough to know that he was the last person who should be in a relationship with anyone. Work took up 85 to 90 percent of his brain cells, leaving precious little to invest in anything more than the friendship he and Evie had always had. Mainly because it had always been light and easy.

At least until one specific night had destroyed any semblance of light. And easy. He and Evie had kissed under the glittering lights of the Las Vegas Strip. She'd looked up at him, laughing at something he'd said, and it just happened. That kiss. It had lasted only a second—a light, playful peck that he hadn't expected to rock him to the core, but it had. And it was a mistake. Because just like the two main characters in the musical they'd just seen, their paths led them in opposite directions.

Dear Reader,

Have you ever been in a situation in which you felt you needed to be the "strong" one? The rock on which other people lean when faced with a life crisis? That's the case with the hero of *Las Vegas Night with Her Best Friend*. Max was the person his father looked to for comfort when Max's mom died of cancer when he was a teen. As an adult, Max is still that way, shunning comfort and appearing as if he can weather any storm. Until his closest friend, Evie Milagre—who's just been through a life crisis of her own—helps him realize he can't and that it's okay.

Thank you for coming along on Max and Evie's journey as they weather the victories and heartaches of working in the medical field. And maybe, just maybe, they'll be able to set aside their personal fears and give love a chance.

I hope you love their story as much as I enjoyed writing it. Happy reading!

Love,

Tina Beckett

LAS VEGAS NIGHT WITH HER BEST FRIEND

TINA BECKETT

MEDICAL ROMANCE

Harlequin®
MEDICAL ROMANCE

Recycling programs for this product may not exist in your area.

ISBN-13: 978-1-335-94275-3

Las Vegas Night with Her Best Friend

Harlequin Enterprises ULC
22 Adelaide St. West, 41st Floor
Toronto, Ontario M5H 4E3, Canada
www.Harlequin.com

Printed in U.S.A.

Three-time Golden Heart® Award finalist **Tina Beckett** learned to pack her suitcases almost before she learned to read. Born to a military family, she has lived in the United States, Puerto Rico, Portugal and Brazil. In addition to traveling, Tina loves to cuddle with her pug, Alex; spend time with her family; and hit the trails on her horse. Learn more about Tina from her website or friend her on Facebook.

Books by Tina Beckett

Harlequin Medical Romance

Alaska Emergency Docs

Reunion with the ER Doctor

Buenos Aires Docs

ER Doc's Miracle Triplets

California Nurses

The Nurse's One-Night Baby

One Night with the Sicilian Surgeon
From Wedding Guest to Bride?
A Family Made in Paradise
The Vet, the Pup and the Paramedic
The Surgeon She Could Never Forget
Resisting the Brooding Heart Surgeon
A Daddy for the Midwife's Twins?
Tempting the Off-Limits Nurse

Visit the Author Profile page
at Harlequin.com for more titles.

To my family. Thank you for being my rock!

PROLOGUE

EVA MILAGRE LOOKED at the first picture in the small stack and blinked. Tried to process what she was seeing. Her last name might mean *miracle* in Portuguese, but right now it didn't look like even a miracle could save her marriage.

"You investigated Brad?"

Her friend on the barstool next to her wrapped an arm around her shoulder. "I'm so sorry, Evie. After you told me his hours had been all wonky and that he'd been evasive about his last overnight trip, it sent up several red flags."

Her gaze didn't waver. The picture showed her husband hugging another woman. A raven-haired beauty that made Evie feel tired and rumpled in her scrubs with strands of hair escaping from her clip and falling wildly around her face. It could be something totally innocent. An embrace after closing a deal at his investment firm. But there was no way Darby would be showing her pictures of her husband hugging another woman if it wasn't something bad. Really bad.

Her thumb hesitated—Evie didn't want to see anything else. "And the rest of these?"

"They're worse. I hoped he'd prove me wrong. He didn't."

Her friend turned toward her, holding out her hand. "I didn't think you'd believe me without those. I know how much you love him."

The thing was, Evie was no longer sure that she did. The pictures just sealed the deal. She handed them back. "And his firm?"

Brad hadn't shown her the financial statements for his business this year, which she found odd as well. He'd always been so proud of what he'd accomplished, going out on his own almost three years ago. When she'd asked about them, he said he was late in filing them this year.

"He filed for bankruptcy a month ago and gave up the lease on his office space."

Bankruptcy? God. He'd been leaving home every single day at the same time, kissing her on the mouth and telling her he'd miss her before walking out the door of their home. She'd heard nothing about any kind of trouble. And she'd put a big chunk of her own money toward him opening that business and had trusted him to…

She'd trusted him. Too much. And it looked like she was going to pay the price for that. Swallowing hard, she bit back tears of anger and frustration. "Thank you. I just can't fathom how he would do something like this."

"I know. I can't believe it, either. We both went to college with the guy, and he was voted the most likely to succeed."

"It looks like he succeeded alright." Her laugh held more than a hint of desperation as her fingers tightened around the stack of photos. "Only not in the area I expected." All she could see in her mind's eye was the woman he was evidently having an affair with. Since they hadn't had sex in the last six months, the reason made far too much sense—he'd used the excuse of work overload and stress, and she hadn't challenged him on it. In fact, she'd been secretly relieved, since she could relate to both of those things. She'd been feeling stressed and tired herself recently, their talks of having a baby going up on a shelf until things settled down. Thank God they weren't still trying. What if she'd been pregnant?

"Do you want to stay with me for a few days?"

A sense of relief washed over her. At least she wouldn't have to face him. Tonight, anyway. "That would be wonderful." She held up her hand for another drink and after the bartender brought it over, she took a gulp of the spiked fruity drink. "I can't promise I'll be in any shape to drive after this." She put her glass back to her lips and drank again.

"Don't worry. I've got this."

"Thanks." She picked up her phone and pushed the button that would connect her with her soon-to-be ex. She wasn't surprised when it went straight to voice mail. She decided to just get it over with. "I won't be home tonight, but when I do come back to the apartment, I expect you to be packed up and gone."

The second she disconnected, her phone rang. It was Brad. She didn't answer. She was pretty sure he would figure out that the jig was up. But she hoped he did as she asked. Because tomorrow morning she was going to head to town, find a lawyer and file for divorce. It was something that probably would have happened, anyway, even without Darby's news. Neither one of them seemed happy with where they were anymore.

Her friend glanced at the phone she'd placed

on the polished bar after silencing it. "Do you think he'll leave without a fight?"

Evie took another drink. "I don't know. I'm pretty sure he has someplace to go, unless she's married, too."

"She's not."

Another laugh came out. "You are nothing if not thorough, Darbs."

Her friend gave her a searching look. "I hope you know this is not how I wanted this to play out."

Now, that was the first thing her friend had said that she took issue with. "You and Max always had issues with Brad."

Ugh. Why had she even said Max's name in the same sentence as Brad's? She and Darby and Max had always been close friends. But something had changed between her and Max when she started dating Brad and they got married. He hadn't even come to her wedding, saying that he had a medical conference to go to. His absence had cut deep. And he'd made it pretty clear, even before the wedding, that he was no fan of her fiancé.

"We both cared enough about you to tell you there were some areas of concern."

Except Max really hadn't spelled out anything specific. He'd just seemed peeved whenever Brad was around. Soon, he'd practically dropped out of her life.

"And yet you never investigated him before now."

"I was a cop when you got married, remember? Running an illicit investigation is frowned on in those circles."

Why was Evie blaming her friend for something she'd gotten herself into? "I'm sorry, Darbs. I had no right to say that."

Her friend's transition from being a police detective to a private investigator had been heartbreaking. A bullet to her leg would have left her friend chained to a desk, so she'd decided to resign and open up her own PI office, where literally chasing down suspects was no longer required. Instead, she chased them via a keyboard or, in Brad's case, through the lens of a camera.

"It's okay." Darby shifted in her seat, barely catching her cane before it fell from its perch. Her limp wasn't as noticeable as it had been years ago, but Evie knew it still hurt when she'd been on her feet too long. "I can investigate now, though. And so don't expect me not to run your next beau through the wringer."

"Next beau? Nope. I think it's one and done as far as that goes."

"Famous last words, Evie."

"Famous or not, they're true." And she meant it. She didn't see herself going down her current path with anyone else. How could she ever trust a man again? First Max backed out of her life, and now her husband. That didn't mean she'd be entering the nearest convent and taking a vow of chastity. It just meant she was no longer going to equate sleeping with someone with being in love with that someone. No matter whom it might be.

CHAPTER ONE

"Dammit." Today hadn't started off well for Maximilian Hunt. He'd gotten numbers back on two of his patients and neither one of those reports had been good. He leaned back in his chair and pinched the bridge of his nose, trying to staunch the vague rumblings of a headache. He could appease the migraine gods by telling himself that neither of those patients were without options. Both had been newly diagnosed and were just starting treatment. But he always hoped for a misdiagnosis that went in the patient's favor, rather than the other way around.

He made a note to call both of them in for an appointment to discuss things. One of his least favorite tasks in his job.

A knock at the door made him push aside those thoughts. "Come in."

The door opened, and Evie peered past it. He could barely see her face.

He hadn't seen her in almost a month. And

it's how he'd hoped to keep it. Ever since Darby had called him to tell him the news a year ago, that Evie's marriage was over and the reason for it, he'd had a hard time not chasing down Brad and letting him know how little he thought of him. The bastard had hurt someone he cared about very much.

But now, Evie was divorced, and she could move forward with her life. Darby had been on him to join them for dinner, like old times before Brad had come on the scene, but he wasn't sure he wanted to go back to those times or seeing Evie every week.

And he wasn't sure why.

Oh, hell, he knew. And that's precisely why he was so reluctant. Seeing her with another man had churned his gut in a way he hadn't expected. In a way he hadn't wanted to dissect. He still didn't.

His college friend opened the door a little farther and frowned from across the room. "Do you mind if I talk to you for a minute?"

"Not at all." He motioned to the two chairs that sat across from him. He did mind. Kind of. But there was no way he was going to say that. Especially not when she sauntered across the room, her hips encased in her snug skirt swaying ever so slightly with every step.

Dammit!

The word from a few moments earlier swept through his skull again, crashing into one side of his brain with enough force to make him wince.

He gritted his teeth and waited for her to take a seat. This was why he'd been happy to see a wedding band on her ring finger. He was attracted to her. Even when they'd been just friends. But he knew himself well enough to know that he was the last person that should be in a relationship with anyone. Work took up eighty-five to ninety percent of his brain cells, leaving precious little to invest in anything more than the friendship he, Evie and Darby had always had. Mainly because it had always been light and easy.

At least until one specific night had destroyed any semblance of light. Or easy. He and Evie had kissed under the glittering lights of the Las Vegas strip after the trio had gone to see a production of *Wicked*. Darby had caught a taxi and gone home, and left Max with Evie. She'd looked up at him, laughing at something stupid he'd said, and it just happened. That kiss. It had only lasted a second—a light playful peck that he hadn't expected to rock him to his core, but it had. And it was a mistake. Because just like the two main characters in the musical they'd just seen, their paths led them in opposite directions. He'd been married to his job. He still was. And Evie was married to… Well, he wasn't sure what she was married to now, but it wasn't Brad. Not anymore. And that made him feel…

Uneasy. Because that kiss had happened just before she started dating Brad. And he sure as hell didn't want things to go back to that time before her marriage. Because he might want to kiss her again. And he would end up hurting her. Just like her ex had. Well, not in the same way, since Max would never cheat, but he also wasn't good relationship material.

And Evie was not a one-night-stand kind of girl. She never had been, and he'd respected the hell out of that. But Max could never give anyone more than that. And he had no desire to change. Life was easier when it was just him.

When she made no move to say anything, he decided to push a little bit. "You wanted to talk about something?"

"More like ask something. I'm kind of desperate actually, but feel free to say no." Her mouth twisted in a way that might have made him smile under different circumstances.

"Desperate?"

"Yes. I've asked several other doctors, but they all turned me down."

For what? Did he even want to know? Especially since his head was imagining all kinds of scenarios. All of them revisiting that kiss from years ago.

"Turned you down for what?"

"The gala."

Hell. The annual hospital fundraising event? She'd always brought Brad in the past and he'd pointedly avoided crossing paths with the couple any more than necessary, other than the cursory greetings he gave most of his other acquaintances. And he'd made it a point never to go to those galas.

"Are you asking me to be your date?" The words slipped out before he'd had a chance to examine them for stupidity.

Her eyes widened as if horrified. "My... date?"

Okay, so that's obviously not what she meant. And he felt like a fool for even thinking along those lines. But did she have to look so stupefied?

Yes, she did. Because it helped him relax into his seat.

Before he could think of a funny rejoinder, not that there was anything humorous about the situation, she quickly added, "I—I wanted to ask for your help planning it."

Did that mean she already had a date? He pushed that question from his head. He was feeling more and more angry with the way this conversation was going.

"I thought there was a small committee that handled the gala every year."

"There was. But Dr. Parker, who normally headed it, moved to Texas to teach at a university there. And the rest of the committee stepped down, saying it was time to hand the reins over to someone else. I kind of fell into the role. And was assured that it was a piece of cake."

"How big of a piece?"

That made her smile. "Like maybe a whole sheet cake. And so far, no one wants anything to do with it. The venue has been the same for the past ten years, so that is already set up. And I'm hoping the same goes for the caterer and so forth."

He was evidently her last stop, since she'd been turned down by every other person she'd asked. So she actually was desperate, although it stung a bit that she acted like she had nowhere else to turn. But still, he wasn't sure he could stomach disappointing her. Especially after the year she'd had. She'd had to sell her apartment and split the proceeds with her ex despite the fact that she'd sunk a bunch of money into his investment firm. According to Darbs, anyway, who told him way more than he wanted to know. It made Max want to step in and fix everything, and he knew he couldn't. Not this time. But maybe this was one area where he could help.

"So what would you need from me?"

"Just to be a sounding board and maybe make some phone calls to past sponsors to see if they wanted to help with this year's gala. I know Darby doesn't work here, and she won't be involved, but maybe we can all meet for din- ner—it'll kind of be like old times. I'm sure she won't mind if we talk shop for part of it."

Was she making sure he knew that they wouldn't be dining alone?

Darby had still been pestering him to join them, and he'd always managed to have some- thing else to do. And he wasn't even sure why. Except that having Evie here in his office was messing with his equilibrium, the way it used to before she'd gotten married. It had to be some weird phenomenon like muscle memory that was coming back to haunt him.

But trying to explain that to her wouldn't be

in anyone's best interest. Because she might think his interest in her was more than just friendship and it wasn't. He wouldn't let it be, because it could only end one way: with their friendship imploding in the worst possible way. Max was not interested in relationships. Never had been. But for now, all he could do was nod and repeat her words back.

"Just like old times."

"So you'll help me?"

"Yes. When is the gala again?"

She snorted. "That's right. You don't attend them."

"Nope. And don't expect that to change, just because I'm helping plan it."

Her head tilted. "Is that a challenge?"

"Just a statement of fact."

She gave a smile that had his libido sitting up and taking notice despite all of his inner speeches. "Well, we'll just see about that, shall we?"

What had she thought she was doing? Max had made it pretty clear that he'd been avoiding her for the last year—actually it had been longer than that—and she had to go and flirt with him?

It wasn't exactly flirting. It was the back-

and-forth repartee they used to have before something had changed. When their friendship was light and easy, and so uncomplicated. Before her marriage.

She'd thought that had been the problem. He hadn't exactly liked Brad, and he'd made it pretty clear once they started dating. Had said that he didn't trust the guy. She'd laughed off his warnings at the time. But, looking back, it was easy to see who'd been the better judge of character.

But she wasn't about to admit that to him. Or to anyone, except for Darby, even though Max had to know by now what had broken up her marriage.

Maybe some part of her was still looking to get back to those earlier times, because they'd been happy. *She'd* been happy. Their little friendship trio. Her and Max and Darby. Her best friends in the world. In fact, at one time she thought that she and Max might even… But then he'd suddenly pulled away, and she'd been wounded deeply. Brad had come along soon after that with his smooth confidence and obvious interest. It had been a balm to her bruised ego. The rest was history. Only instead of bringing back Max, it had seemed to push him away even further. But then she'd gotten married and with the business of life had been able to push the friendship to a back burner. Until now. There'd been a reason that he was the last person she'd asked to help her with the gala, and she had fully expected him to refuse.

Only he hadn't.

She laid her head on her desk and groaned, letting the cool surface of the wood absorb some of the embarrassment over that coy smile she'd sent him as she'd stood to leave his office. She hadn't meant anything by it. But what if he thought she did? If she'd been hoping to mend fences with him, that was probably off the table now.

Her eyes tracked up to look at the clock on her wall. Time to get back to work. She had a busy day ahead of her. Especially now, since she'd just bitten off more cake than she could possibly chew. And there was a staff meeting at three with the hospital's new CEO about the gala. He wanted all department heads there. Evie wasn't a department head, but because she was now in charge of planning the event, he'd sent a memo specifically asking that she be there. So she would. Maybe the meeting would even land a few more volunteers to help with the planning.

* * *

Max's headache hadn't let up and he'd barely made it to the smaller of the two conference rooms before Arthur Robbins, the hospital's new CEO, got up to speak. He slid into his chair and caught sight of Evie sitting a short distance away. She hadn't noticed him yet, since she was talking to someone to her left, and it gave him a chance to properly study her. She was a little thinner than she'd been a year ago, probably due to the stress of the divorce. But it was good to see her smiling again. She hadn't seemed happy in…a while.

And how the hell did he know that? Because while he might not have been chummy with her over the last few years, he still found himself noticing things about her when he did see her. And the last year of her marriage with Brad had found her smiles few and far between. She'd become serious and focused on her work. Kind of like Max. Not that that was a bad thing. But Evie's personality used to be geared more toward being happy and lighthearted. She'd always had a witty rejoinder. But those had practically disappeared.

He'd glimpsed a bit of that lightheartedness just as she was getting ready to leave his office after asking him for help. She'd thrown him a look and a grin that had shifted something in his chest.

Dr. Robbins got up and received a smattering of applause as he took the podium. Max shifted his attention from Evie to the man. Robbins had once been a plastic surgeon and although he was in his mid-fifties, he could easily pass for early thirties. And with his easy smile and confident bearing, he was probably the perfect person to take on the role after Morgan Howard had retired last year.

"Thanks for coming. I've gotten to meet most of you in person over the last several weeks, but for those of you who don't know me, I'm Art Robbins, and I look forward to working alongside you to make this hospital reach its highest potential."

Something about the way he said that made Max shift in his chair. Was he saying the hospital had lacked something under the last CEO? Morgan Howard had been much loved, his compassionate nature evident in almost everything he did.

Robbins went on to talk about the gala and how he'd looked at the figures the event had brought in over the last several years. "And there's no denying they're solid numbers, but I feel they could be even better with a little work.

I'd like to thank Eva Milagre for heading up the committee. A committee that will make this the best event in this hospital's history."

The man had mangled the pronunciation of Evie's last name, making *Milagre* somehow rhyme with *pedigree*. And yet, when Max glanced her way, she hadn't moved in her chair.

"But we can only make it the best if we all plan our schedules so that as many of us are there as possible. After all, it's a party, and who doesn't like to attend a good party?"

Had Evie gone to the man and complained about him not attending the party in the past? Had that been what the smile in his office had been about? Whatever part of him that had been moved by it hardened to stone.

"And it *will* be a party, but I'd also like to think of this as a work event. Where we can go and mingle with prospective donors. Having faces to put with the names people see listed in the hospital's foyer is always a good thing. I really want to see those donations double or even triple this year. So I want each of you to pick up a flyer and a sign-up sheet that I have up here at the front. Please encourage your folks who aren't scheduled to work that night to attend if at all possible. Again, look at it as a work event, just like the meeting this morning."

Although the man smiled as he said the words, had Max sensed a vague threat hidden in there? When he glanced at Evie again, she was staring back at him, giving him a slight shrug. He had no idea what that meant. But he planned on finding out. Just as soon as this meeting was over.

Fifteen minutes later, it was, and he went up and got the flyer and sign-up sheet while the CEO was in conversation with someone else. He waited at the back of the room and watched Evie go up to the man and shake hands with him as if sealing a deal. He tensed further before ducking out of the room and waiting for her to appear. When she did, he struggled to keep his tone civil as he asked her to join him for coffee. She glanced at him, blinking as if surprised at the request, but nodded. Once they were in the cafeteria, seated with their cups, he studied her for a second before saying anything.

"Was Robbins's speech for my benefit?"

"Wh-what?"

"You know, talking about everyone needing to attend the gala. It's never been a requirement before and we both know it. Is that what you meant when you said 'we'll just see about that'?"

There was a long pause and then understanding dawned in her eyes. "No, of course not. My saying that was a joke. I had no idea Robbins was going to talk about any of that today. I'm as shocked as you are. And for your information, I don't agree with making it a required work event. It used to be looked at as part of the perks of being a staff member, that you could get dressed up in your finest clothes and have fun and eat a fantastic meal on the hospital's nickel. I think what he's done will kill the spirit of the event."

So she hadn't put him up to it. Now, Max felt like a jerk for even thinking it. He knew her better than that. At least he used to think he did. Was he just searching for reasons to be mad at her? If so, that wasn't fair to her.

"I'm sorry, Evie. I think I'm just looking for someone to blame and you happened to be a convenient target."

"It's okay."

He reached across and touched her hand, the warmth of her skin immediately waking up something inside of him. Pulling away, he smiled. "Thanks, Evie."

"Not a problem. And I hate to bring it up, but is there a good time when we can meet to talk about some of the specifics? I can ask Darby to come and we can make a night of it, if you want. But if staff is going to be, er, *encouraged* to attend, then our guest list just increased by about a hundred people from what we had last year. Robbins also wants me to try to increase our pool of sponsors by at least fifty. So that brings the guest list even higher."

"Maybe you should have told him you'd do that as soon as he learned how to pronounce your name."

She laughed. "I'm used to it."

Max lifted one eyebrow. "I remember being schooled on how to say it when we first met."

Her nose crinkled in a way he found adorable. "Because people who are my friends and family should be able to pronounce it."

Even after she'd gotten married, she'd kept her last name, just hyphenated it for documents. But at work, she'd always just been Dr. Milagre. He assumed if he and Evie had gotten married she would have done the same.

That pulled him up short. They weren't married and never would be, so it was a moot point. "Speaking of meeting to talk about logistics, most of my evenings are free." He didn't exactly have a big social calendar, and although he dated casually from time to time, there was no one in the picture at the moment. "And I'll see if I can come up with a list of people who might want to attend the gala as sponsors."

"That would be great, Max. I'll text Darbs and see what dates she has available." She stood. "I have an appointment in a few minutes, so I need to go, but I'll touch base later this afternoon on possible meeting times and places."

That was the third time she'd mentioned inviting Darby. Was that her way of saying that she was uncomfortable being alone with him? He was probably reading too much into something that he should be thankful for. Because she might not be worried about them being alone, he sure as hell was, and he wasn't sure why.

"Sounds good."

With that, she disposed of her trash and headed out of the cafeteria, leaving him at the table to mull over his options as far as avoiding going to the gala. From what Robbins had said, there were no options. And since he had patients of his own to see, he waited for the elevator Evie had gotten into to close its doors before he headed out there himself.

CHAPTER TWO

"HELLO, MRS. COLLINS. How are you today?"

"Okay, I guess." Even as Evie walked in the door, though, she could tell that one of her favorite patients was not okay. She was struggling. It was there in the increased rise and fall of her chest and in the breathlessness with which she'd said her words.

"Is your inhaler not working?" Margaret Collins had been Evie's patient for several years. She had controlled asthma, so it was odd to see her breathing so out of whack.

"It's been taking more puffs from it to get things back to where they should be."

Evie frowned. "Have you been sick recently?"

"No, which is why this is so weird. I feel fine otherwise."

"Why don't I give you a quick once-over first."

A list of possibilities scrambled through her

head, each trying to make itself heard. Blood clot in the lungs, COVID and pneumonia were among the top choices.

She looked at the vitals her nurse had taken and then listened to the woman's chest sounds. Her left lung sounded clear, but when she listened to the right, she heard decreased breath sounds. And her pulse was hovering on the low end of the nineties. It didn't exactly knock any of her potential ailments off the pile, but it did shift them slightly. "Are you okay if I call for an X-ray?"

"Yes, whatever you need to do. I trust you."

She heard that a lot from patients, and she understood where they were coming from. But she also wanted them to trust their bodies. To know when they weren't working the way they should be.

Evie called down to Radiology to see if they had an opening and it turned out they did. Normally, she had to wait for a slot to become available. Since Margaret was her last patient before her lunch break, she opted to walk her down there and get her signed in. "Once they get the results they'll call and let me know, and then I'll get in touch with you, okay? I don't want to prescribe additional medications until we know what we're dealing with."

"I just want to be able to catch my breath."

"I want you to, too. We'll work on that."

"Sounds good."

Evie walked out of Radiology and headed for the cafeteria. She got her food and sat down, glad to be off her feet. She saw Arthur Robbins on the far side of the room and wished she had opted to go to one of the local coffee shops instead, but she was here now. And maybe he wouldn't even notice her. Right about then, his gaze swung toward her and he gave her a quick wave before rising and heading her way.

Oh, great. She wasn't really in the mood to hear about anything gala-related, but since she was in charge of it, she probably didn't have much of a choice. And it had been almost a week since the staff meeting, so he probably wanted an update. That was too bad because she'd called the venue where they used to hold the gala and while they said they could accommodate the projected hundred and fifty extra attendees, they couldn't add anyone else without them being over the fire marshal's limits. Which would mean they might have to find a new venue and, if so, they would lose their hefty deposit on this one. Maybe she could talk Dr. Robbins out of the new requirements and ask him to institute them next year instead.

After all, then people would have more notice, since the gala was in two months. She was pretty sure trying to find a new place in that condensed period of time was going to be nothing short of a headache.

He stood over her table with a fixed smile on his face. "How's the planning coming?"

It was now or never. "I have some concerns that I'd like to talk to you about. Is there any chance of setting up a meeting?"

"My schedule is pretty tight right now. Can you give me a quick rundown?"

She did as best she could after being put on the spot.

"So what I hear you saying is that the current venue can handle our projections of a hundred and fifty extra guests."

"Yes, but—"

"We'll simply limit the number of tickets to that number and leave it at that."

"And if that leaves some of the prospective donors out in the cold?"

His smile widened, but the man didn't look pleased at being pressed. "From where I'm standing, Nevada isn't looking too chilly these days. Besides, invitations to last year's donors have already gone out and we've asked them to RSVP by next week. That should give you a rough number and you can go from there."

Not *we*, but *she* could go from there. There was one more thing she needed to run by him. "Okay. Also, our previous CEO did the welcomes and so forth, so I wondered if you'd be carrying on with that tradition."

"I wouldn't miss it. I'm working on my speech even as we speak."

Actually, there was something chilly in Nevada. Their new leader. Whereas Morgan Howard had been warm and welcoming, Dr. Robbins seemed cool and aloof. And he wanted this year's fundraiser to double or triple in donations?

She forced a smile and thanked him. He then walked away to another table, that same smile firmly in place. Maybe she was misjudging the man, but something about him made her edgy. She couldn't read him like she could Howard. Somehow, unless he was a very good actor, she didn't think his persona was going to foster a lot of new interest in giving to the hospital. If anything, Evie was fairly certain that donations were going to be down unless the doctors themselves could make those connections. Maybe that's what Robbins was counting on and why he'd instituted the new attendance requirement.

Maybe that's also why no one else wanted to be on the committee. Had the man's reputation preceded him? Evie didn't usually listen to the hospital's gossip chain, but maybe in this instance she should have tried. Because if something didn't change, this gala could wind up being a colossal failure. And she could see that failure being dropped right in her lap. Not that she couldn't take a little criticism. But she loved this hospital and wanted it to get the funds it needed to grow and help more patients.

Her phone pinged, and when she glanced down, she saw it was the hospital's radiology department. Wow, that was fast. She'd just left Margaret down there less than fifteen minutes ago. She answered the phone and waited as the tech gave his findings.

The results made her close her eyes and let out a long shuddering breath. "Okay, thank you for letting me know. Is Mrs. Collins still there?"

"No, sorry. We sent her on her way. Did you want us to keep her?"

"No, it's fine. Thanks again." She disconnected and sat there, her lunch untouched as she tried to process the one possibility she hadn't put on her list.

Margaret Collins had a mass in the lower lobe of her left lung.

Max waited for Evie to arrive at his office, just like she had a week ago. But this time, she'd given him advance notice and said it wasn't about the gala. But her voice had been strained in a way that said she was worried about something. Something involving a patient.

Since Evie was a pulmonologist, her concern was probably related to a finding during a test. And that she suspected a tumor or she wouldn't be running to him with it.

He remembered when his mom had been diagnosed with cancer. She'd come home and said she needed to talk to his dad alone. Because of the way she'd said it, he'd stood outside the door and listened, horrified at what he was hearing. Brain cancer? That couldn't be right. He'd burst into the room, a thousand questions in his mind and his eyes burning with tears.

His dad had sat motionless at the dining room table, and rather than being there as a support for his wife, he'd lifted a bottle of what Max later knew to be alcohol and drank deeply from it while his mom comforted them both. She had told them it would be alright, that the doctors had a plan and she'd be starting chemo in less than a month.

In the end, his mom hadn't had a month. Her tumor had hemorrhaged and she died on the operating table. And his dad hadn't stopped drinking. Not during her short illness and not afterward. He remembered checking the bedroom before going to school to make sure his dad was still breathing. Max, who was still grieving the loss of his mom, had been suddenly thrust into the role of caregiver, a job he neither wanted nor felt capable of. But it was either that, or end up an orphan. So he coaxed his dad to eat and put him to bed when he was too drunk to get there on his own.

And in that time, Max had decided that he was going to help people like his mom, because in doing so, maybe more people wouldn't wind up like his father, a shadow of the strong person he'd once been.

The knock at his door drove him from his thoughts. "Come in."

Evie entered and this time she didn't wait to be asked, she just sat in one of the chairs. She had nothing in her hands, but that didn't surprise him, since all of the patients' records were now kept in an automated system. So there was no need to tote around physical X-rays or paper records. "I have a patient who I think has cancer."

"Give me her name."

He looked up the chart and went through the findings. "No MRI yet?"

"No, just the X-ray. I expected it to show pneumonia or something different, but not this."

"I get it. I take it she's gone home."

"Yes. And is waiting on my call."

"I'll need a biopsy to know for sure. But I want to do an MRI first to get a better look at whatever this is. Do you want me to make the call?" He wasn't sure why he asked that. It would be protocol for Evie to contact the patient and let her know that she needed to be seen by an oncologist. But he sensed something in her demeanor that said this was going to be a hard one. Besides, she had come directly to him rather than writing up an order that would land on the desk of one of his office staff, who would then call him to set up an appointment.

She paused for a minute as if thinking about it. "No, she's my patient. At least for now."

"She'll always be your patient, Evie. I'm only treating one part of her."

"So am I. But she's...a special one, even though none of my patients are supposed to be any more special than the others."

He was right. He'd always been good at reading Evie. Even during that quick kiss all those years ago, he'd sensed that she wanted something more from him. Something that he couldn't give her. Not just because he was afraid of ruining their friendship if something went bad. But because of his dad and how he'd become after his mom died. He'd become a shell of himself and had never recovered. Max had seen many partners lose loved ones. Every day a new one walked through the door of his office. But if Max didn't have a partner, he couldn't lose them. Couldn't grieve his way into a pit of despair.

He knew that kind of thinking was skewed, but he'd already lost two parents. And he'd lost his dad long before he'd died of cirrhosis last year, right before Evie and her husband split up. Max's soul felt as dry as the drought that was currently afflicting Las Vegas. It had been months since the last bit of rain had come their way and severe water restrictions were currently in force.

Evie was looking at him strangely, and he

realized his thoughts had wandered for longer than he'd realized.

He stood up from his desk. "Do you have time for a walk out in the courtyard before your next patient?" He hadn't been much of a friend since her split from her husband, and if he wasn't careful, he was going to do exactly what he'd told himself he was trying *not* to do: lose her friendship.

"Thanks. I'd like that."

The relief in her voice said he'd done the right thing. "We can talk about the gala for a few minutes and kill two birds with one stone."

Except Max wasn't sure what the first bird was, except maybe the fact that he'd missed her. Had missed seeing her on a regular basis. Had missed laughing with her and going on their dinner dates and excursions with Darby. They still hadn't had that dinner she'd mentioned about planning the gala. Or had she decided she didn't need his help after all?

"Good. Because the venue the hospital usually uses can only accommodate a certain number of folks, and by requiring that staff go, Dr. Robbins is reducing the number of potential donors that can attend. It's one of the reasons that in the past, staff was invited but attendance wasn't required. I do get why they want department heads there, though."

He stood, waiting for her to do the same, his eyebrows going up. "Ah, so you think I've been remiss in my obligations by not going."

"Not remiss." She smiled. "Just antisocial."

That made him laugh. Because she knew him. In an even deeper way than Darby did. Darby had actually gone to medical school for a year or two before realizing the health-care field wasn't for her and had made the leap to the police, much to the dismay of her parents. She'd breezed through training. Had been the maid of honor at Evie and Brad's wedding, and then been wounded in the line of duty a year later, opting to resign when it became clear that her leg would never regain full function. But she seemed happy with what she was doing and claimed that there was nothing better than being your own boss.

Max was beginning to see the benefits of that after the doozy of a staff meeting they'd had. He'd even toyed with opening his own practice. But he loved hospital work. Loved working with other specialties—seeing the *life* that ran through this place. Oncology could be rewarding, but it was also draining and heartbreaking at times. The atmosphere at the hospital helped mitigate those aspects of his job.

Even the gala was probably not the onerous chore he'd made it out to be.

"So how do you plan to balance the staff-to-donor ratio?"

"I saw Robbins in the cafeteria and when I mentioned my concerns, he basically batted them back at me, saying he wasn't worried." One of her shoulders went up. "I'm hoping the sign-up sheet will give me a better idea of what we're dealing with. It's kind of short notice to say that everyone has to go. There are people who've already planned vacations and so forth. He did say that exceptions could be made for those folks who absolutely couldn't come."

"Hmm…maybe I should plan a vacation for that time."

"No way, chum. You know that you never take actual vacations."

It was true. Both Darby and Evie had gotten on him about that. He did take time off. But he almost always stayed home and didn't do anything special unless it was dinner with her and Darbs. Even when his dad died, he'd only taken off the day of his funeral. And he'd looked stiff and awkward whenever anyone approached him. But, Evie being Evie, she had

said she got why he was that way. He'd told her
the story about his dad's drinking and when it
had started.

She also got why he abstained from alcohol
and had always been her and Darby's designated driver. At least until he'd stopped coming to their dinners. Things had never been the
same between the three of them since then. But
now—with the gala—maybe he had a chance
to rectify that. Unless—like the medications
he prescribed—he decided that the risk out-
weighed the benefits. The jury was still out
on that one.

They found themselves out in the large courtyard. The space was carved out of the middle of the medical center. It could only be
accessed through the hospital. There was no
lush greenery out here. Just interesting rock
formations dotted with succulent plants and a
central sculpture. But the place had a beauty of
its own, just like the desert, as triangular sun
sails and the tall walls of the hospital provided
shade over a multitude of seating areas. And a
flagstone path wound through the space, giving patients and staff alike a spot to contem-
plate their day. It was really lovely, and at night
there were countless strings of fairy lights that

gave it a beautiful, romantic appearance. Several staff members had even held their nuptials under those lights.

Max glanced around. "Too bad this space isn't being used for the gala. It would give visitors a chance to actually see the hospital and know where their dollars were going."

Evie cocked her head. "Actually, it probably would be big enough. It must be at least as big as the ballroom at the hotel. Tables could be set up throughout the space and a sound system could take care of making sure everyone could hear what was going on. But I don't know if it's possible to cancel the reservations at the hotel."

"If not this year, then maybe next year."

"Yes…"

She seemed to see the space with new eyes. And he loved watching her mind work. It was there in the way she perused her surroundings, in each twitch of those full pink lips. In the way her head tilted ever so slightly to the left.

He couldn't help but stare.

Since Max had never attended the event, he had no idea what the atmosphere was like, but surely the hospital could match or even surpass whatever was done off campus at these events. And with catering and being able to rent almost anything, right down to tablecloths and silverware, surely it was doable. Although no one could guarantee the weather would cooperate. But with rain looking like more and more of a luxury right now...

"I think it would be lovely. An intimate setting, rather than the formality of an elegantly appointed hotel. We could still erect a temporary dance floor from wood planking in the far left corner, where we have benches arranged in that large circle."

That area was often used as a venue for small lectures or for students and their families who were touring the hospital, hoping to be accepted into one of the local universities. They could visit and chat with other students, as well as staff who would talk about the hospital. So it was already set up as a gathering space, just not for the size or scale of a large event such as the gala.

She glanced at him with eyes that were bright and expectant. "Would you be more apt to come to the gala if it were held at the hospital?"

"Since it's now required, isn't that a moot point?"

"But what if it wasn't? What if this were any other year and held on the hospital grounds."

He thought for a minute. "Then, yes. Because I know that I could always go hide in my office if I got too bored."

"Exactly. I think more staff would want to come. Especially if they knew they could escape to either the staff lounge, the café, or any of the other waiting-room areas. They wouldn't be confined to a table or any one space. They could mingle and visit with each other the way they can't when they're at work. I think it would be a win-win. For everyone."

"You might be right." In fact, she probably was right. "The question is, will Robbins go for it?"

"Ugh. He's kind of a wild card. All I can do is come up with a plan and try to sell it to him. Do you think you could draw up a replica of what such an event might look like?"

She remembered that he liked to sketch? It shouldn't be surprising. During that awkward period after their kiss, he'd wanted to make up for his weird reaction, so he'd drawn a scene from *Wicked* from memory and had wrapped it and sent it to her house. She hadn't said much about it, but she had come up to him the day after she got it and had looked in his face, and simply said, "Thank you." But he could tell she was touched by the gesture. It helped them get past that terrible phase that could have turned terminal. He was grateful that it hadn't.

Was thankful he still had her friendship, even if he had been remiss in nurturing that over the last year and more. But like he'd thought earlier, maybe he could make up for that. At least a little. And as a friend, he could do this for her.

"Send me a list of what you want included in the drawing and I'll see what I can do. I can't promise it'll pass muster with Robbins, but maybe it'll give him a hint of what such an event could be like."

"Thanks, Max. I truly mean that."

He smiled. "I'm happy to do it."

"One more thing. If you have time in the next week or two, I'd like to call the hotel and see if they'll let us look at the venue. I was there last year, but don't remember exactly how things were laid out, since I wasn't involved in the planning. Maybe they'll even have pictures of what the room looks like set up. And I can walk out here in the courtyard and do a comparison, to see if we can fit buffet lines and the number of tables we'll need."

He glanced around before a thought came to him. "The courtyard opens to the atrium area of the hospital. Its size makes a big impression, with high ceilings, and it's not cluttered with a lot of furniture. We could spill over into it. Or maybe even set up the catering area in there. And I bet we could get some fans set up in strategic places to help keep things cool, although once the sun goes down that shouldn't be a problem."

"True." She smiled and gripped his hand, giving it a squeeze. "I'm liking this idea more and more. In fact, maybe we can even use it this year. We could have the formal part of the gala at the hotel and then have something set up in the courtyard, where people could come once that's over, if they want to see what the hospital is like. Something informal juxtaposed against the stiff formality of the event itself."

It was all he could do not to press the hand she'd squeezed against his pant leg to erase the feeling of her warm soft skin against his.

"I think Robbins would go for that. He has to have actually liked the hospital to have accepted the position as CEO of it. Surely he'd want to show it off?"

"I agree. And maybe that will make the idea of having the gala in house next year more appealing. That, along with the beautiful rendering you're going to draw."

One side of his mouth went up. "No pressure, though, right?"

"Oh, I'll press as hard as it takes to make you say yes."

And what if she'd pressed the night of that kiss all those years ago? What if she'd pulled him closer and deepened that kiss. Would he have taken her home? Carried her to bed and stayed there with her the entire night?

Not something he wanted to think about right now. Especially not with the way she was looking at him. As if he could do anything.

It's just a drawing, Max.

He needed to remember that, before he started ascribing personal motives to something that was anything but.

She pulled a pad out of her pocket and scribbled some notes on it. "Before I forget anything," she muttered.

Was she talking to him or to herself? A minute later she ripped the small sheet off and handed it to him. "It's just some of the things that I thought could be included in the drawing. If I think of anything else over the next few hours, I'll send you a text, okay?"

He perused the list. She wasn't kidding when she said she didn't want to forget anything. Ambiance, dance floor, seating that included tables and comfortable groupings of nice chairs, DJ station, food tables, bar, open doors to the atrium, additional strings of lights…

He sent her a grin. "I don't think we could fit anything else out here if we tried."

"You don't think it's over-the-top, do you?"

"I think this CEO is expecting exactly that. So, no." He glanced at the list again. "I'll start working on this tonight and hopefully have it to you within the next couple of days."

"That would be perfect. Thanks so much, Max."

"My pleasure." And it would be. He'd felt badly about what Brad had done to her, but hadn't known what to say or do to help her get over that. Instead, for the last year, he'd pretty much walked the other way whenever he caught sight of her. Not because of Brad, but because of himself. And he couldn't think of anything more selfish than that. Maybe he had a little more of his dad in him than he liked to think. The only thing he didn't do was drink.

Maybe it was time to make up for that lapse. And if a simple drawing would help, then he'd do ten of them.

"Oh, and about your patient with the mass, I'll let you know when we set up the appointment, if you're interested."

"Yes, thank you. I'd like to be there for the consult, if it works with my schedule. That is if you're okay with that."

"Yep. Not a problem at all."

"Great." She pocketed her notebook and glanced at her watch. "Speaking of patients, I'd better get back to it."

"Me, too. Talk soon."

They parted ways, and he realized he was looking forward to talking to her, even to collaborating with her on the gala. And he wasn't sure if that was a good thing or something that would come back to bite him. But he'd worry about that if and when it happened.

CHAPTER THREE

"Wow. You weren't kidding when you said you'd get me something in a few days."

He'd placed a large drawing of the courtyard against the wall and was now standing across from her, watching as she perused his work. Her office was slightly smaller than his, and although he had been in her space before, it was different this time somehow. And she wasn't sure how she felt about it. It reminded her so much of the time he'd gifted her that drawing from the play they'd seen, and even though this wasn't the same thing at all, it still brought back all of the emotions and feelings that receiving that gift had elicited. Especially since it had come after that disastrous kiss. And right before he seemed to go AWOL from their friendship.

And maybe it was because he'd been absent for so long that his very presence seemed to overwhelm the space...and her. Not so much with his size, but his sheer magnetism. It was there in his raw masculinity, the scent of his soap or shampoo or whatever he used, and, of course, those green, green eyes that made her want to get lost in them. She'd always felt that way about him no matter where they were. He'd always been a big part of their trio of friends. So his absence, especially over the last year, had been sorely felt. In fact, even when she'd been married to Brad, Max had been hit or miss as far as being there because she knew he hadn't liked her ex.

But at the time, his withdrawal had made processing that kiss a little easier. Made the realization that nothing would ever come of it a little more bearable, despite the tremendous hurt she'd felt. Because back then, she'd nurtured a tiny bit of hope that things might evolve from there. But he'd apologized and said he didn't want what had happened to affect their friendship. Except that it had. It was then that he'd started making excuses about why he couldn't go out with them. Not always, but enough that she deduced that it was because of her and what had happened. Darby had even asked about it, and although Evie was pretty sure she knew the reason for it, she didn't want to admit it. Didn't want her friend's sympathy over something that couldn't be changed.

She'd realized she had to make a life for herself. She couldn't go on mooning after a man who'd never had a steady girlfriend and had made it clear that he wasn't the marrying kind. Evie was. Brad had proved that. Or at least she'd thought he had, until Darby had presented her with those awful photos. The aftermath of her and Brad's breakup had been just as awful. He'd hounded her for two months, trying to get her to change her mind. And once he realized there was no going back, he'd turned nasty and had sued her for half of her earnings, forcing the sale of their apartment.

She'd lived in Darby's spare bedroom until the divorce was final. Three months in all. Only then did she feel like she could get her own place without worrying Brad would somehow come after that, too. Only now did she feel like she was starting to recover from the trauma of that time.

With everything that had happened, she saw some wisdom in Max's aversion to relationships. And Evie could say she was now firmly on the side of Team Single. And she wasn't about to change that anytime soon.

She forced her mind back to the drawing

when she realized she was staring sightlessly at it. Moving closer, she crouched on the floor across from it and took in what he'd done.

How had he gotten so much detail into it?

The courtyard space had been divided into four different zones. A section for hors d'oeuvres and drinks was right off the entrance to the foyer of the hospital. Rather than the buffet tables she'd envisioned in the atrium, he'd put romantic lighting on each table and drawn in waitstaff carrying trays of champagne and canapés.

Off to the left were the benches that were already in the space, but Max had put small side tables where people could talk and place the food and drinks they'd carried from zone one. It looked like he'd had potted plants brought in to give at least a small illusion of green space, and give people hope that there might be rain in the near future, even if none was forecast at the moment. A shortage of water was a very real concern in this part of Nevada. And there was no relief in sight. Just more sunshine and blistering summertime temperatures.

Fortunately, once the sun set, cooler temperatures moved in, which was one reason Sin City had such a booming nightlife. The gala setting looked like any one of those fancy resorts that were packed into the city. Only this had a vibe that was more intimate. A vibe that encouraged confessions…and maybe even huge donations. She glanced at Max for a moment before returning her attention to the canvas. The only colors on the otherwise black-and-white rendition were the faces of those populating the drawing. While featureless, those faces gave the appearance of life and warmth. And she loved it.

The third zone was the dance floor that they'd talked about. Twinkle lights hung overhead and lined the edges of the low wooden platform that appeared to be made out of hardwood flooring. On it, couples floated across the space in all of their finery.

"You're making me nervous." Max's low voice vibrated over her, causing her heart to skip a beat or two. "You're not saying anything."

"Because I'm blown away by it. All of it. This is beyond fantastic. If Dr. Robbins doesn't go for the idea, then I'll be shocked. Oh, and I like that you left the last zone as a strolling path."

There was one couple holding hands as they walked past the huge sculpture and rock formations that were in the area. It opened up a pit in her stomach that made it hard to breathe for a minute. Because she could imagine Max and herself in place of the pair in the picture. But it wasn't true and never would be. Because the fact of the matter was, she would stroll that path alone. Brad had betrayed her and Max hadn't wanted her.

The hurt from the past rose up all over again and threatened to swallow her.

But she wasn't really being fair to Max. He didn't want anyone—it wasn't a rejection of her in particular. And if she was smart, she would get rid of whatever vestiges of romantic notions she might harbor for the man before she lost him again. She'd been enjoying having him back in her life over this last week—she could see how it had been an impetus to start moving forward again after a year of feeling stagnant and unwanted.

And now she felt wanted again? Ugh! She hoped she wasn't pinning her self-worth on how Max acted or didn't act toward her. If she did that, she'd just end up pushing him away again. Besides, those feelings weren't real. They were from not having anyone in her life right now. Maybe she should think about dating again. After all, Brad had been gone for a year and even if he came groveling back, she didn't want him—would never be able to trust him after what he'd done.

"I thought after the meal at the other venue, people might want to move around a little bit to burn some of it off."

She forced a smile, glanced back at him and stood. "And holding hands as they do. That was a romantic touch."

He gave a half shrug, part of his smile fading. "Purely a selling feature. Just like the couples on the dance floor."

"Ah, I see. Because Max Hunt doesn't have a romantic bone in his body."

She wasn't sure why she said it, especially in tones that were a little more waspish than necessary as evidenced by the muscle that was now pulsing in his cheek. Probably feeling guilty over her thoughts from a minute ago, she sighed and added, "Sorry. That was uncalled for."

"No, it's okay. I can wish romance on others, even if I don't want any for myself."

"You don't think you'll ever be involved with anyone?" And there she went again. She wasn't asking for herself—at least that's what she told herself. She just thought Max deserved the happiness that came with companionship. Despite the way that she and Brad had ended, she had been happy with him for most of their marriage—even if it was more a comfortable feeling of familiarity rather than a rush of chaotic emotions that she had trouble sorting out. At least with Brad she'd known what to expect. Well, except at the end.

He gave her a quick glance before looking away, but not before she caught something almost poignant in his expression. "I don't think so. My mom's death was hard on my dad. He became someone I no longer recognized and I'd really rather not go through something like that."

"Not every partner dies so young."

"No. But in my family's case that's how it happened. And the process leading from her cancer diagnosis to her passing is something I'd rather not put any kids I might have through."

Her head tilted. "And yet you became a cancer doctor."

He didn't answer for a second, but finally he nodded. "It was because of my mom. But that doesn't have anything to do with my not wanting a serious relationship. The fact of the matter is that I like my life the way it is now and I don't want to risk that over something that might not—that probably *won't*—last. After all, look at you and Brad."

"Wow, okay. I get it. It's none of my business."

He closed his eyes. "Sorry, Evie. I didn't mean it that way. I'm just trying to show that even when you think something is going to last forever, it doesn't always. I try to live my life honestly. And don't ever want anyone to get the wrong idea and be hurt because of something I've said...or done."

Was he warning her off? If so it wasn't necessary. She'd gotten his message a long time ago. "I get it. I'm really not interested in a relationship, either. Like you said, there's me and Brad."

He was silent for a moment, then she felt warm hands on her shoulders. He gave her a light squeeze before letting her go. "I'm sorry, Evie. That man deserved worse than what he got. And you deserved better."

He evidently knew her ex had tried to take her for everything she had. Probably from Darbs. Thankfully, once the divorce was final, he moved away with the woman he'd been seeing. She had no real idea where he was right now and had no interest in knowing.

She took out her phone and snapped a shot of the picture as a way of changing the subject. "I'll send this to Robbins. Can I keep the drawing in my office, in case he wants to see the original?"

"Of course. I thought maybe you'd want some tweaks."

"Are you kidding? This is a masterpiece. It's perfect the way it is. But don't be surprised if it goes up on the wall of the hospital somewhere, or if our new head guy ropes you into doing some other drawings."

"Nope. I only do them for a few special people."

And Evie was one of those people? All of her self-lectures from moments earlier flew out the window and in their place something warm and tingly stirred in the pit of her stomach. She had to bite her lip for a minute to stop the sensation from spreading. The last thing she wanted was for Max to realize how much those words meant to her. So she again changed the subject. "Any news on Margaret Collins?"

"The patient you referred to me?"

"Yes."

"I actually have an appointment scheduled with her for this afternoon. Do you still want to be there?"

She thought for a moment. It wasn't absolutely necessary that she attended. Margaret would be in good hands, since she trusted Max implicitly. But she would like to be. Would that seem odd to him that she would want to support her patient?

"I don't want it to seem weird or for you to feel like I don't trust your judgment."

"Why would it seem weird? Family members sit in all the time. As her pulmonary specialist, it makes sense that you would want to know what her treatment will be so that you can help carry it out."

When he said it like that, it didn't sound strange at all.

"Thanks, Max. I'll take you up on that then. What time is her appointment?"

"At three thirty. Are you free then?"

"I should be. My appointments tend to be in the morning. And I do a second set of rounds in the afternoon. So I'll just pop over to the appointment and then come back."

He nodded. "Speaking of popping over, I hadn't meant to stay as long as I did, so unless you have any other questions about the drawing, I'll head back over to my office."

"No questions, just a huge thank-you. I'll let you know what Robbins says."

"Great. I'll see you around three thirty, then."

Speaking of which, she needed to write that

down before she forgot. Not that she was likely to. Her insides were already doing loops at the prospect of seeing him again so soon. Talk about a downpour in the midst of a drought. It had been a long time since she and Max had spoken so freely to one another, and she was going to turn her face up to the rain and enjoy it while she could. And ignore the fact that, like living in the desert, the rain wasn't likely to last.

As the day went on, Max became less and less sure about having Evie sit in on Mrs. Collins's appointment. There had been something unsettling about being closed in her office while she studied his drawing, especially since she'd asked him about whether or not he might consider being in a relationship.

Had she even realized that she'd used a fingertip to trace the couple he'd drawn who'd been walking together in the picture? He had shuddered, as if she'd been running her fingers along his skin rather than an inanimate object. He still hadn't gotten that image out of his head. When he'd kissed her in front of that theater, her palm had curled over the back of his neck. The warmth of her skin against his had served to jerk him back to awareness just as the mental image of them in bed had slid through his brain.

That same image had risen up as she'd touched that drawing, the intimacy of the act making him picture them together all over again. It made his nerves prickle to life, along with another part of him that needed to be kept on a short leash. Before something bad happened. Not that sex was bad. And with her it was guaranteed to be good. Very, very good. But it couldn't happen if he had any hope of salvaging their friendship—a friendship that was just now being brought back online.

Was the burst of lust something remembered from their past? There'd been that same shivery sensation that he'd thought he'd banished long ago. Or was this something entirely new? If so, he needed to put it in the past and leave it with his other baggage. Because if he couldn't...

Well, then there would be no more meetings in anyone's offices and no more collaborations on anything work-related or not. And the friendship that he'd hoped to salvage would be dead in the water. Again.

His phone pinged and his emotions went on high alert until he glanced at the reading and saw that it was Darby. He immediately relaxed and read the text. She'd actually written the word *squee* followed by an absurd number of exclamation marks. The message went on.

Evie texted me a copy of your drawing and I love it. She said she's headed to the CEO's office to show it to him. He's going to go berserk. If he doesn't, then he doesn't deserve to run that hospital.

That made him smile. He couldn't picture Dr. Robbins going berserk about anything unless it was something related to dollar signs. He texted back.

Don't get your hopes up too high. He's not the most demonstrative man, from what I've seen of him.

Was he sad that Evie hadn't asked him to accompany her to the CEO's office? He'd be lying if he said no. But he'd also hinted to Evie that he had a busy afternoon ahead of him. Maybe she was afraid Robbins wouldn't like his plans, despite what she'd said. Except that Darby had also seemed to think his rendering was worth presenting to the man.

His phone pinged again.

Well, I think this will float his boat. Besides, he'd be crazy not to go for this. It'll give him a chance to show off his hospital to potential investors. I can't wait to hear what he thinks.

He smiled.

Thanks for the vote of confidence.

Once Darby signed off, he was left with a strange sensation. He had no idea what had caused it or why it was so unsettling, but it was. It could be that it was better for him not to be there. Because he didn't want to witness the sense of disappointment flit across Evie's face. He'd already lived through that once before and didn't want to go through it again. If only she knew that he'd saved her from a relationship failure that was as bad, if not worse, than what she'd gone through with Brad.

Oh, he wouldn't have cheated on her, except with his job. And he certainly wouldn't have gone after her money. But he knew himself well enough to know that he would be withholding some of himself. It was a defense mechanism that he'd brought into play while he was taking care of his dad. Oh, he'd taken care of his physical needs, but he'd felt powerless to help him with anything more than that. Because he'd expected to someday come home and find his dad dead, either by drinking himself to death or worse. Thankfully, it hadn't come down to that. He'd just damaged his liver beyond repair instead. That damage hadn't shown its face until Max was long grown up and out of the house.

The damage done to Max emotionally, back then, hadn't reared its head until later, either. Until he'd started thinking about Evie in ways that had nothing to do with friendship. It had paralyzed him and made him realize something inside of him was missing. Something that had to do with him trying to meet someone's needs in a way that went beyond the physical joining of two bodies. Because he knew that was all that he'd be able to give her. And she'd eventually come to hate him for it.

He shook his head and stood up to stretch his back. He needed to go do something besides just sit here and think about the past. Or about Evie. He glanced at his watch. It was lunchtime, so he might as well go out of the hospital. Maybe he could throw off some of his thoughts. Besides, he was pretty certain he would find out what Dr. Robbins thought of the ideas soon enough. And they weren't even his ideas. They were Evie's. All he'd done was put them to paper. So he'd go and eat and sit somewhere where his thoughts would not be consumed with hospital stuff.

So, he headed down the street, hopefully leaving the clutter in his head far behind.

Margaret Collins looked relieved, which struck Evie as odd. She would have expected her older patient to be defeated by a possible cancer diagnosis, but she didn't seem fazed. "Evie, dear, I'm so happy you were able to come."

She'd said it as if it was a birthday party or some happier occasion. An inkling of worry erupted in the back of her head. She'd never known her patient to think with less than a clear head, but this sounded… Well, it didn't seem like a normal reaction.

When she glanced at Max, she saw a troubled frown. Evidently she wasn't the only one to find Margaret's words odd.

"I thought Dr. Milagre should be here so that she'd know what treatment your tumor needs and would be able to know how to treat the breathing aspects."

"Of course. I never meant anything other than that. She's just always been so sweet to me, even before this, when I had COVID and no one knew if I'd live or die. But Dr. Milagre never seemed to have any doubts." She glanced at Evie. "You were always so encouraging and your sense of hope was contagious. It still is, which is why I'm glad you're here."

Evie's concerns eased. "Your willingness to follow a treatment plan and to never stop fighting played a major role in your recovery. I'm counting on that same determination to get you through this as well."

At seventy-two years of age, some might have not wanted to put the woman through cancer surgery or chemo, but other than her asthma, Margaret had always been remarkably healthy. At least from what her records said and what Evie herself had seen. She was an amazing woman, and she reminded Evie of her own grandmother, who'd come over from Brazil and had made a home in a new place with her family. She'd lived to the ripe old age of ninety-six. And if COVID hadn't come along, her grandma might still be alive. But instead, it had taken her life, even while sparing Margaret's. She sincerely hoped her patient had another decade or two to live.

"We're going to do an MRI today and get a better look at what we're dealing with. We'll inject a little dye into your system to see how much of the tumor is being fed by your blood vessels. Then we'll schedule a biopsy. Do you have family who can come and take you home from that, since you'll need anesthesia to do the procedure."

"My son can. He lives a few miles from my place. The only reason he's not here today is because I didn't tell him. Not yet, anyway. I wanted to have a better idea of what I'm facing before bringing anyone else in my family into it."

Max perched on a stool in front of her and looked her in the eye. "You're going to want to call him for this one."

"You're that sure?"

"Sure enough. I really want someone here for you. There will be a lot of information thrown at you in a short amount of time. It would be good for someone else to be a second set of ears. No one remembers everything."

He was right. After Darby had shown her those pictures of Brad, her mind had been a mess and she'd barely remembered anything said afterward. It hadn't been a medical emergency, but she'd still been glad Darby had been there for her and had been her support system. She'd even come with Evie when it came time to tell her parents what was happening. Her dad had threatened to come for Brad, and at least give him a piece of his mind. She and Darby had talked him out of it, eventually convincing him that it wouldn't change anything and could only make things worse.

Brad hadn't been worth it. He still wasn't.

"I'll ask him as soon as you know for sure that it's cancer."

Max laid his hand on Margaret's. "We won't know that for sure without the biopsy."

"But you'll have a better idea of what it is with the test today, right?"

"We should have."

Margaret nodded and turned her hand over to squeeze his. "If the test seems to indicate it is, then I'll tell him."

"Good."

"Then let's get this show on the road then, shall we? The sooner we know, the sooner we can get this thing out of my chest. Or at least I'll hope that we can."

Max turned to look at Evie. "How is the next hour looking for you?"

"I can't think of anywhere I'd rather be." She quickly added, in case Max got the wrong idea, "Than with you, Margaret."

The older woman swiped her fingers under one of her eyes before glaring at them both. "These damned allergies…"

Allergies or not, Evie was glad she could be here for Margaret, no matter what the results turned out to be.

She hadn't had time to even tell Max that Dr. Robbins had loved the sketch and had agreed, even on such short notice, that they should incorporate the ideas into this year's gala. They would still do the speeches and appeals at the hotel ballroom, but they would shorten that portion of it to an hour or two, enough to serve dinner and get through the fundraising portion. But then they would invite everyone over to the hospital to enjoy some desserts and drinks. Robbins had gone so far as to say they would hire a taxi service to drive those home who had imbibed more than they should have. And this way, staff members who were on duty would be able to pop into the courtyard for a few minutes and at least get a few refreshments.

So while Margaret was getting her MRI, she thanked Max again for the drawing. "He's giving us everything we wanted."

His eyebrows went up. "Maybe he's not as hard-nosed as he seemed. And since people can come and go as they please once they get to the hospital, there shouldn't be a problem with overcrowding."

"No. There shouldn't. They're going to rotate some board members and have them take people on tours of the hospital, so it won't be everyone out in the courtyard all at once."

His eyes focused on the images going across the screen as they were taken. He swore softly.

"What is it?"

"It's hypervascular," he said, pointing at the tumor. "And I'm pretty sure it's metastatic, probably from her breast, liver or somewhere else. An angiosarcoma."

"Oh, no." Her whispered words were part prayer. An angiosarcoma was a rare cancer and Max was right—lung involvement almost always originated from somewhere else. Which meant it might have also metastasized to the brain or other organs. "Will you still need a biopsy?"

"To be one-hundred-percent certain, yes. But if it's what I think it is, it'll be aggressive."

"I know." Evie's heart plummeted and all of a sudden fundraisers and whether or not they got to hold part of the gala on hospital grounds seemed so unimportant.

"I want to stay while you tell her."

He nodded. "I figured as much."

They helped Margaret down from the MRI table. She looked at their faces. "It's bad news, isn't it?"

"It's not the best."

"I see." She stood there for a minute before sitting gingerly down on the wheelchair they'd used to bring her into the room. "Are there treatments?"

"Yes. Chemotherapy and possibly some radiation. But we don't think the lung is the primary site. We think it came there from somewhere else."

She twisted her hands in her lap. "Oh, my. That is bad news, isn't it?"

"Like I said, I still want to do the biopsy. And it's time to bring your family members in on this and let them know what's going on. You mentioned your son lives nearby."

"He does. I have a daughter, too, but she lives in Maine at the moment. That's such a long way to travel…"

"Why don't you let her decide if that's too far or not."

They wheeled her to Max's office and Evie sat beside her and held her hand as Max continued to give her more information.

Margaret interrupted once to ask how soon he'd want her to have the biopsy.

"As soon as possible. We'll want to begin treatment right afterward. Will your son be able to stay with you?"

"He's married with three teenaged daughters. How can I ask him to do that?"

"I understand. But I have to be honest. You'll need support during treatment. I won't lie and say it'll be easy, because it won't."

She gave him a frank look. "Is it even worth it, in your opinion? If this were your mom, would you suggest she go through chemo?"

He paused for several long seconds and Evie's heart contracted. She knew the story of Max's mom and it was a heartbreaking one.

"My mom never got the chance to go through chemo. Her cancer was found too late and she died before she could start treatment. But to answer your question, yes, I would want her to at least try one course to see if there was any improvement."

"I'm sorry about your mom. She must have been a special lady, because you're a good man."

Max smiled. "Well, some might argue with that assessment."

He glanced at Evie, his mouth twisting sideways. Did he think she was one of the people who might argue with that assessment? Not on her life. And she was going to make sure he knew it. Just as soon as his appointment with Margaret was over.

CHAPTER FOUR

"Do YOU THINK I don't think you're a good person?"

Max frowned. The question had come right on the heels of his patient leaving the room. "What? Where did this come from?"

"When Margaret said you were a good man, you looked right at me when you said there were people who might not agree with that assessment."

"I'm sure that was a coincidence." It hadn't been, though. He had looked at Evie, but he just hadn't realized she'd caught the movement. Until now.

"I'm pretty sure it wasn't." She took a step closer. "You are a good man. Why would you even think otherwise?"

"You're reading too much into all of this." His heart thumped hard a time or two before going back into a normal rhythm. She was standing just a foot away from him, her head tilted up to gaze at him, the brown of her eyes soft and knowing. As if she knew all of his secrets and was hell-bent on prying them from him one by one.

"Am I?" Her hand went up to touch his face. "Is this because of your mom? You were only a kid back then. You couldn't have stopped what happened to her."

"I know that." A coil of emotion unspooled from somewhere inside of him. "There are days, though—days like today—when I wonder why I went into a specialty that is rife with so much heartbreak. Margaret is probably not going to survive this, you know."

"I know. But if it goes into remission she could have some good years ahead of her. Years when she'll be able to see her grandkids grow up and live her life to the fullest. That has to be worth something, despite the heartache."

Her fingers were still touching him, moving over his jawline in a way that made him shudder. And dammit, he needed this. Needed to feel something other than the desperation of all of the Margaret Collinses of the world, although she seemed remarkably at peace with whatever might happen.

"Evie..." He closed his eyes and balled his

hands by his sides to keep from gripping her arms and pulling her closer. Much closer.

"It's okay, Max. You don't always have to be strong."

He felt arms go around him and her cheek pressed against his chest. She was hugging him. Hell, she was only trying to comfort him. So why did the urges going through his body right now have nothing to do with comfort? Or hugging?

But he did have to be strong. Because to be anything other than that would be dangerous. Not just for him, but for Evie, too.

He opened his eyes and looked down at where she was pressed against him. And God help him, his arms went around her and hugged her close, one hand sliding up into the silky strands of her hair and gripping it.

A tiny sound came from her throat, and at first he thought he was holding her too tight and was hurting her. But then he realized it wasn't about that. It was something else entirely.

His hands went to her shoulders and eased her away, and Max looked down into her face as he did. Her eyes, rimmed with impossibly dark lashes, were moist with emotion, and suddenly he knew there wasn't enough strength in the world to stop him from doing what he was about to do.

Except before he could even make a move to do exactly that, Evie went up on her tiptoes and pressed her lips to his in a kiss that was as soft as a butterfly's wings and as deadly as a cobra's strike. Because it ignited a maelstrom inside of him that took over all rational thought. And soon, the kiss was anything but soft. His hand went to the back of her head and held her as his mouth covered hers, his tongue sliding between her lips only to be welcomed home as she opened to allow him any and all access. And he accepted her invitation, his palms going to her back and sliding down until her hips were pressed firmly against his. And this time, the sound she made wasn't imagined. It was real, very real, and if this went much further she was going to be on his couch and rolled under his body until there was nothing separating them, and they could...

Hell, no. She didn't deserve this. Didn't deserve someone that would just take what she was offering and give nothing in return. Because even as his body clamored for it, his mind knew that was all that would be in it for him.

He pulled his mouth free. "Evie. Stop... please."

She tried to move closer again and this time he somehow summoned some superhuman strength and set her away from him. "We can't."

Evie stared at him for a second, the back of one of her hands pressed against her mouth. Then she straightened, her fingers going to her hair and dragging through the mussed locks.

"We can't what, exactly?"

He motioned to his couch, letting the bald implication speak for itself. He didn't want any warm fuzzies entering the conversation and muddying the waters. Hell! She'd tried to argue that he was a good man? Well, he was about to disabuse her of any such thoughts. Because what he'd been thinking had been the opposite of good or noble.

She frowned. "You think I was angling for you to sleep with me?"

"Weren't you? Because that was sure the direction my thoughts were headed. I'd be damned surprised if yours weren't there as well."

They stared at each other, both of them still breathing hard. Then she shrugged. "So what if they were? We're both adults. It's not like I'm asking you for a ring." Except there was a quick flash of pain in her eyes that cut him to the core.

God, he didn't want to hurt her. Had tried so hard over the years to keep from doing exactly what he was doing now. "Evie, I know you aren't. But I just can't give you what you deser—"

She took a step back. "Don't! I know all of the blah blah blahs you're about to recite. You're not the marrying kind. You don't do relationships. You don't want forevers. You'll remind me *again* of how Brad and I wound up. Well, let me let you in on a little secret, Max. I did learn something from my marriage, even if you think I didn't. I'm not after any of those things. Not forevers, not declarations of love, not emotional pleas for more than you can muster." She sucked down an audible breath. "So your overinflated opinion that anyone who sleeps with you must immediately fall head over heels in love with you is way off base. But just in case you're still worried, let me make it as clear as I can. You won't have to turn down a night of pleasure with me ever again. Because this truly was our last dance."

Is that was she thought? He gave a hard laugh. Because if he was worried about anyone immediately falling in love with someone, it was the other way around.

"Something funny?"

Only then did he realize how that had probably sounded to her. But there was no way he could explain that he wasn't laughing because of what she'd said. It was because the reality of those "blah blah blahs" she'd named was still true. Even after all these years.

Rather than respond, he just shook his head.

"Perfect. Well, I guess that about sums it up for both of us." She turned to go, and then said over her shoulder, "Please let me know when Margaret's biopsy is scheduled. I want to be here for it."

As much as he wanted this conversation to be over, he didn't want her to leave like this. "Evie—"

She stopped him with an uplifted hand. "Don't worry. This won't affect our professional relationship. Or our friendship. I know that was another one of your arguments the last time we kissed. But we got through that…kind of. So we can get through this, too."

"Wait."

She turned back and stared at him, eyebrows raised as she waited for him to say something else. But for once his brain was blank. Because what could he say? Everything that she'd just thrown at him was true.

He shook his head. "Nothing. Except, I'm sorry."

"Well, don't be. Because I'm not. See you around the hospital."

With that she was out the door, leaving him to wonder if she would ever speak to him again. Because despite what she'd said, he couldn't think of any way that this wouldn't affect their friendship. Not this time. Because this kiss wasn't the same as the last one. Not in any way, shape or form. It was way worse. Because it had meant something. If not to her, then to him.

Darby nudged her leg under the table. "What is wrong with you?"

"Nothing."

"No. Don't even try that stuff with me. It doesn't work. Since Max conveniently had surgery tonight—*again*—and said he couldn't make our dinner, I take it he's the reason for those slumped shoulders."

Yes, he was. But Evie honestly didn't know how to fix it at this point. When he'd laughed at her for saying that she expected her to fall in love with him if they slept together, a scorching pain had ripped through her. Because it might have been true. If they slept together she probably would fall for him. He'd helped her see what a huge mistake that would have been. But along with the pain, there'd been anger. Furious words had tumbled around her brain, and she'd had to grit her teeth before she lashed out and used them to cut him to the ground. Instead, she'd stormed out of his office like an indignant child.

But now that she'd had time to think, she realized she'd overreacted and hadn't given him a chance to say anything else. Because she'd been scared. Scared he would avoid her like he had the last time this had happened. And it looked like he was. Even Darby could see it for what it was.

She decided to come clean. "I kissed him and he seemed to kiss me back. Until he wasn't and started backpedaling so fast that things became a blur of anger and regret. I'm pretty sure that's why he's not here."

Darby's mouth fell open and her eyebrows shot up, reaching near her hairline. "You kissed *him*?"

"Well, I mean, I think he was about to kiss me, but then I just kind of…beat him to it."

She tried to put her thoughts into words. "It just happened. I'm not even sure why or how."

"Wow. Did you guys talk about it?"

She shrugged. "I talked at it. And around it. And through it. And then I stormed out of his office."

"You didn't." Her eyes rounded. "I know it's not funny, but I'm picturing you slamming his door behind you. That is not like you. At all."

"I know." Her chin dropped into her hand and she probably looked every bit as miserable as she felt. "But I don't know how to repair the damage."

"You go and talk to him again. And again. As many times as it takes for him to screw his head back on straight. I know the guy has a thing against commitment, but from what I'm hearing, you didn't ask for one."

"Correct. I don't want one. I don't know that I'll ever get married again after what happened with Brad. But he even threw that in my face."

"God. I can't blame you for storming out, then. Maybe we'll all just be groovy old singletons when we turn seventy."

Although Darby had nothing against marriage, she just hadn't met the right person yet. And after one failed engagement, it didn't seem like she was in a hurry to change her status on social media.

"Maybe. And you're right. I probably do need to go talk to him. The kiss was just impulsive. It meant nothing. I just need to get him to understand that."

"That's probably a good idea." Darby reached over and squeezed her hand. "Plus, it's hard to do the planning for the gala if you end up being the only one on the committee. And since part of the event will now be held at the hospital, there's a lot of last-minute things to organize, like caterers and DJs and linen services, right?"

"I know. I'll try to talk to him. And if that doesn't work, I'll have to find someone else who'll be willing to help out."

"He'll come around. He probably just feels awkward about everything right now. You could try to reschedule dinner, but until things are resolved between you two, it's probably just going to be lather, rinse, repeat, with him finding excuses not to come."

Although Darbs wasn't trying to make her feel guilty, she just felt more and more miserable as dinner went on and ended with her just picking at her food.

"You need to go home, Evie. Get some rest. Things will probably look better tomorrow."

Her friend was right. Even though Max was avoiding her at the moment, she couldn't really see him not following through with what he'd committed to do. He wasn't anticommitment in general, just when it came to relationships.

They paid their bill and then headed out the door. She turned when she heard her name murmured in a low, familiar tone. Shock made her stand completely still.

Max was standing there in black jeans and a turquoise polo shirt, looking completely at ease. And completely gorgeous.

Oh, Lord, what did he want?

She couldn't think of a single thing to say, just stood there looking at him like an idiot. It was Darby who broke the silence. "Sorry you missed dinner. I hope your emergency worked out okay."

One side of his mouth quirked. "The jury is still out on that. Sorry about tonight, though."

It was then that she realized he wasn't talking about his supposed surgery, but about what had happened between the two of them. She didn't think she could hash it out in public like this, though. It was one thing to tell Darby in confidence, but to then have things laid out like his surgical instruments?

Thankfully, Darby again saved the day as she leaned on her cane and said, "Well, I've got an early morning, and my leg is giving me fits tonight, so I'll say good night."

"See you later. I hope your leg feels better," Evie replied, giving her friend a hug.

Darby whispered, "Good luck" in her ear.

Ah, so it wasn't the leg giving her fits, she was just giving Evie a chance to talk to Max alone. He was here, so he must be ready to talk things through, right? Or maybe he was coming to say "sorry, but I can't help you with the gala after all."

Darby had caught a cab and was on her way home, leaving her and Max standing in front of the restaurant.

"Walk with me?"

"Okay."

They started down the street, heading toward the Vegas strip, where some of the most famous Las Vegas casinos were located. They strolled in silence for about five minutes before he spoke. "I don't like the way we left things the other day."

A sense of relief swept over her. "I don't, either. And I'm sorry for stomping off the way I did. I really do value our friendship and don't want to lose it over something stupid." She hesitated. "I feel like the last time this happened, you avoided me for a long time, and it hurt. And I missed you. Can we just forget that any of this happened?"

She'd spoken the truth. She had missed him. And it had hurt. Hopefully he would take those two things at face value and accept them for the apology that it was meant to be.

"I missed you, too. And I realized when I had to make up a story in order not to come tonight, then I was headed in the wrong direction. Again. I'm sorry, Evie."

"I'm sorry, too. So we're good?"

"We're good."

Her eyes closed and a feeling of gratitude washed over her. She wanted to hug him but was afraid it would ruin things if she did. So she simply smiled and thanked him.

"So do you want to give me a rundown about what still needs to be done for the gala?"

"I actually wasn't sure you were going to continue on the committee, but I'm glad you are." She pulled a list from inside of her purse and showed it to him. "Anything spark your interest?"

He pointed to an item on the list. "I actually know a guy who DJs for a living if that would help. Nothing off the wall and I think it would fit in with the atmosphere Dr. Robbins is going for."

"You mean cold and cranky?"

Max laughed. "I have to admit, that's a fair assessment. I bet his bedside manner was phenomenal."

"I bet. But at least he liked our idea. If it works out, he thinks we might be able to have it completely at the hospital next year. We can use the atrium for dinner and the presentations and then the courtyard for the after party."

"He actually called it an 'after party'?"

Her mouth twisted. "No. He called it a 'greet and mingle.' But, anyway, if you know a DJ, that would be great, if he's available for the time slot we need him for."

"Which is…?"

She thought for a second. "The actual gala starts at seven and Dr. Robbins wants it to go until around eight thirty. Then those who wanted to would all head over to the hospital. We're thinking that most will want to if we advertise that there will be dancing and a bar."

"So from eight forty-five until, say, eleven?"

"That sounds about right."

He made a note in his phone. "I'll call him in

the morning and let you know for sure. Now, what else?"

They went through the rest of the items with Max selecting a few more things from the list. "Does that help?"

"Absolutely." She paused for a minute as something struck her. "Is Margaret's biopsy tomorrow? I was afraid that was the surgery you were talking about."

"No, I would have let you know if it was tonight. It's tomorrow at ten thirty. Her son will bring her in at six to do pre-op stuff. And then we'll go from there."

"Did her daughter fly in?"

"Yes, she did, actually. I was proud of Margaret for calling and asking her to."

"Her kids are great. I've met both of them over the years."

They stopped to wait for the light to change, signaling they could cross the street. "Having a great support group will help a lot. She's going to need it, if the biopsy tells me my suspicions are right."

"The hospital also has support groups for those with different types of cancers. I'll encourage her to try some of them out. I'm sure she will find one that she likes. It'll help if there are some familiar faces in the infusion room."

They crossed the street and found themselves in the middle of a large throng of people waiting to get into one of the shows. They moved to the outside of the cluster, skirting it as best they could. Maybe they should have gone a different way. But she actually loved the crowds and the liveliness of Vegas. Just by walking its streets, no one would ever guess that there was an unprecedented water shortage going on right now. Except for the hotel notices that had been posted saying that for those staying for extended periods, they would only change linens and towels once a week, things were pretty much business as usual.

"I'm sure she will. And she has a great treatment team behind her, too," Evie said. She meant it. Max and his staff were good at their jobs and their reviews showed it. Not that Evie herself put a lot of stock in those things. After all, anyone could have an off day and either be shorter than necessary with a patient, or too cautious when it came to treatment.

"Well, thanks for that. But she has a good doctor in you as well. If you hadn't found that mass on her lung, who knows how long it would have been before it was found. You may very well have saved her life."

"Well, mutual admiration society aside, let's keep on trying to save her life."

"Not a question. We're all going to fight hard for her." He glanced down the street and then back at her. "Do you have room for some ice cream from Delacort? It's just ahead."

She smiled. "Are you kidding. Delacort is my favorite spot. Their raspberry sorbet is to die for."

"I remember. I also remember the one time they ran out of it."

She laughed. "That wasn't one of my finer moments."

"You weren't rude. You just looked like you were going to burst into tears."

He remembered that? "Well then, let's hope they have some tonight, for both of our sakes."

He laughed and the sound sent a shiver over her. Maybe because she hadn't been sure she would ever hear it again. The urge to link her fingers through his made her curl her palm into itself until it was a fist. She wasn't going to risk doing anything that could be misconstrued. Especially not right after they'd kissed and made up.

Ha! No. Kissing could also be misconstrued. Even figurative kissing.

Instead, she took a deep breath of cool dry air and let herself enjoy simply being with him.

Delacort was a few stores ahead and although Vegas wasn't particularly renowned for its ice cream, it should be, she mused. Or at least this one store should be. It was churned fresh every day and if you happened to go in while they still had their machines going, the place was filled with wonderful scents of cream and sugar and the various flavorings.

The line wasn't too long and they were soon back on the street with their selections. Max's was in a little bowl, while her raspberry sorbet—which, thankfully, they had plenty of—was scooped into a chocolate-lined cone. The tip of the cone was also filled with chocolate and was so good when taking the very last bite of the confection.

"Yum." She took a small bite, and the fresh taste of fruit melted on her tongue, leaving it wanting more. "How's yours?" She glanced at him to see him smiling at her obvious enjoyment of her ice cream. "What? I don't get over this way very often. So it's a treat when I do."

"I know. And mine is as good as it always is."

"I can't believe you don't want it in a cone. But you never have, have you?"

"No. I never have. I like the ice cream all by itself."

Heading back the way they came, she happened to glance to the side and gasped before she could stop herself.

"What?"

"Oh, nothing. I just didn't realize that *Walter Grapevine* was showing here in Vegas."

"Walter who?" He looked so puzzled that she had to laugh.

"It's an off-Broadway musical I've been wanting to see. I was hoping it would come here."

"I've never heard of it."

She wasn't surprised. "It's a smaller production, but it's gotten rave reviews."

"I'll have to look it up."

The topic gravitated back toward the gala as they walked back toward the restaurant.

When they got there, he glanced at her. "Did you drive?"

"No. Darby and I both took a cab together— why?"

"I'll take you home."

"You don't have to. Really, Max, I'm out of your way."

He gave a light shrug. "Only by a few minutes. It's not a big deal."

The parking garage was just a block from the restaurant. Max paid the attendant and they waited as the car was brought up to them. "I'm sorry you ended up having to pay for parking when you didn't even get to eat."

"I had Delacort's finest. I can't complain."

She smiled. "Thanks again, Max. For being able to get past what happened."

"I could say the same for you."

The rest of the trip was made with the kind of small talk that Evie had missed. They talked about work and the gala, and just life. She gave him the address of the apartment she'd bought just after selling her and Brad's previous one. It was just a mile away from where she'd lived before and, despite the anger she'd felt at the time, she was thankfully free of memories that might have plagued her if Brad hadn't needed the funds from a quick sale. It had worked out for the best. And she was happy with the new place.

He pulled into one of the guest parking spots and turned to face her. "I'll let you know tomorrow about the DJ either before or after the biopsy."

"Sounds good. I have an appointment tomorrow after work to go look at the venue, just so I can see the space and find out when it'll be open to us to get the setup done. From what I can see we have a linen service, caterer, someone to set up the sound and a florist coming in. I'm pretty sure I understood that those companies were already contracted last year during the previous gala, but I want to make sure none of those changed. And since last year's coordinator moved to a new hospital, I'm not sure how much he can help us."

"Do you want me to come with you?"

"Do you have time?"

"I do. When does your shift end?"

She had to stop and think a minute. "Five o'clock or whenever I finish my rounds."

"How about if we meet in the lobby at five thirty? You can let me know if you get hung up."

"That works. You'll let me know, too, if it doesn't work?"

"I will."

With that, she said goodbye and stepped out of the car. He made no move to back out of the spot, so she started to walk toward the lobby of the apartment building, feeling his eyes on her with each step. He was just being polite, but it made her self-conscious, something it shouldn't have. Evidently, things hadn't gone completely back to the way they were before, but all she could do was give it time and hope that each day would bring a new sense of normalcy and friendship.

CHAPTER FIVE

SHE WAS UP THERE. Max could sense it. He didn't even need to look. He'd caught a hint of movement in the observation room around five minutes ago. She'd been held up with a patient right as the procedure was starting, but by the time he'd placed the camera for the video-assisted thoracoscopy he would use to perform the biopsy, he knew she'd made it.

He made the other two incisions he would use for his instruments and got back to work. They'd know pretty quickly what they were dealing with and if the mass was benign, he might even be able to get it out during this session. If it was malignant, they would need a PET scan to see where else it was and to help them figure out a treatment protocol.

Watching the screen to his right, he made his way to the tumor and used the grasping tool to hold a section of the lung while cutting off a small piece, then quickly moved in to cauterize the area. The danger with vascular tumors was they could hemorrhage, filling the surgical field with blood. Fortunately, it looked like he'd gotten all of the vessels. After pulling the sample free, he dropped it into the collection cup one of the nurses brought over.

"Can you get that over to the lab?" he asked, although he really didn't need to. She would know what to do.

"On my way."

Now, it was a waiting game to see if he closed her up or removed the tumor. This time he did glance up and saw he was right. Evie was up there. She nodded to him and he returned the gesture before turning back to his patient.

He had a piano concerto playing on the speakers, which was usually his music of choice during surgical procedures. It was soothing, with no distracting words to get tangled inside his head. Every surgeon had their own playlists, or none at all. He had one or two colleagues who wanted it completely quiet.

Ten minutes later, the nurse returned with a name. "Metastatic breast angiosarcoma."

Damn. There were times he just didn't want to be right. This was one of those times. He wasn't going to take the tumor out. And depending on the results of the PET scan...

Well, he would cross that bridge when he came to it. She would need to be in the hospital until the chest tube came out, probably a couple of days. And he would need to go out and talk with the family members who had come to the hospital. He knew her two adult children were here, but had no idea if Margaret had living siblings or not.

He glanced up at Evie and shook his head. Her eyes closed for a minute before she opened them and acknowledged his gesture. It was a damn shame that it couldn't have worked out in their favor. But you had to play the cards you were dealt. He'd learned that the hard way when his mom was taken from him. And then again when his dad drank himself into oblivion.

Both he and Evie were aware that with every patient who came across their paths, there was the possibility that a life would end and that there'd be nothing they could do to stop that death. And Max hated this part of the job. He hated even more that this patient was special to Evie, and that there was nothing he could do to change her odds of survival.

He checked to make sure there was no bleeding before he inserted the chest tube and withdrew the instruments he'd used to take the biopsy, then closed up two of the holes with a stitch or two and tightened the opening where the tubing was to keep it secure.

Then he made sure she woke up from the anesthesia without any problems before he started to head out the door. Margaret reached up with a shaky hand and squeezed his, making him swallow hard. He squeezed back. "I'll come check on you once they get you in your room, okay?"

She nodded, but didn't say anything. Not that he expected her to. He wouldn't tell her the results of the biopsy until she was truly awake and could understand what was going on around her.

Evie met him at the door. "You were right, weren't you?"

"Yes, but it doesn't make it any easier."

She leaned her shoulder against his for a second. "You're doing what you were trained to do, Max. You're not responsible for whether or not it's a good outcome."

Evie's voice was low and soothing, and he realized she was trying to comfort him. Shades of what his mom had done with his dad filtered through and he stood up straighter. "You don't need to tell me what I already know."

As soon as he said the words, he clenched his teeth. "Ah, God, I'm sorry, Evie. It just bites that things like this happen to people who don't deserve them."

"I know. And you don't have to apologize. I was trying to talk to myself as much as I was you. I wished for so much better for Margaret."

"We might not be able to take away the diagnosis, but we can do our damnedest to make sure her treatment gives her the best quality of life possible. I've never believed in extending life just to extend it, though, if those months are going to be lived in misery. I wouldn't want it for myself and I don't want it for my patients."

"I'm in complete agreement, Max."

"Do you want to come with me while I talk to the family?"

"Yes. Her kids will recognize me, and I went to Thanksgiving dinner at their house after Brad and I… Well, my parents were in Brazil visiting extended family at the time, and I didn't want to be alone so I accepted their invitation."

And Max had been too busy trying to avoid her—to avoid the complicated feelings that came along with her divorce—to recognize that she might have been lonely during those first holidays without her ex. She'd been staying with Darby, so he'd just assumed... He sighed. "I haven't been a very good friend, Evie. I don't know why you put up with me."

Her head jerked to look at him. "I didn't say that to make you feel bad. It was more to let you know that I have a history with this family."

"I know. And somehow, that makes it worse. I'll try to do better."

She smiled. "You are. Just don't disappear from mine and Darby's lives again, okay?"

"I won't." It was a promise he hoped to hell he'd be able to keep. Especially as he'd made an impulsive purchase yesterday evening. He wasn't sure what he'd been thinking, or if she'd even go with him. He could always offer the other ticket to Darby and let them go together. But he truly wanted to make it up to Evie and he couldn't think of a better way to do that than to offer her something she loved. And while Darby had liked *Wicked*, she'd confessed that musicals really weren't her thing.

They got to the waiting area and presented a united front when talking to Margaret's family, telling them what they knew so far—that this tumor was aggressive and they needed to find out where else it might be hiding before coming up with a treatment plan.

When her son asked if this was terminal, Max nodded. "I'm afraid so, but I can't give you any more information until we've done some other testing."

As soon as those words were out in the open, brother and sister embraced, with Margaret's daughter breaking into tears. Evie went over and hugged each of them, then promised they would do all they could to keep Margaret comfortable.

After they left the room. Max stood in the hallway for a minute, his own eyes burning before he said, "I do have some more patients to see and I want to check on Margaret. What time is our tour of the venue?"

"At six, so we can meet in the parking lot at five thirty, like we planned. I can drive, or we can catch a taxi, whichever you prefer."

"You drive?" He gave a half snort. "The last time I was in a car with you, you nearly killed us both."

Her eyes widened. "Because some jerk came through a red light and nearly T-boned us. It was my quick thinking that saved you from being squashed like a bug."

"A bug, eh? Quite the opinion you have of me, Dr. Milagre."

"Just stating the facts."

It should seem strange that they could joke after that meeting with Margaret's family, but sometimes inviting some lighter moments in was the only thing that kept him going in the midst of difficult diagnoses. And he was thankful Evie had played along rather than chase the sadness that was Margaret Collins's case.

"Wow." It was the only thing Evie could think of to say as she stood in the cavernous room that would house the initial part of the gala. "It's hard to comprehend how big this room is when it's full of tables and chairs and decorations."

"It is pretty big." Max stood there, his hands shoved in his pockets, and glanced around. "I can see why they chose this place."

"Yeah, me, too."

Right now, the room was devoid of anything except for scaffolding, which was set up in the middle of the room. Some workmen were hanging what looked to be paper lanterns from the ceiling.

With walls that were off white with just a hint of green, the space was bright and airy, a large chandelier giving it an opulence that the hospital's courtyard couldn't match. But maybe it didn't have to. The two places had a completely different feel, but the hospital space would perhaps come across as somewhere that everyone could let their hair down and shrug off the cares of the day. Heaven knew that's what Evie used it for on an almost daily basis. In fact, as her divorce was dragging out, she'd spent many hours out there on one of the secluded benches, needing time to find herself again.

But getting away from the hospital grounds was proving to be nice, too. Margaret Collins's diagnosis had been heartbreaking, something that would haunt her for a while if the PET scans came back with the cancer in multiple places. At least here she could think about something else for a little while.

Really? Then why was it still running through her mind? She did her best to shake it off.

"I think I remember the buffet tables over on the right by the door. Probably because that allowed things to be refilled without staff having to drag food and drink carts through the seating areas."

"That makes sense," he said.

Movement out of the corner of her eye caught

her attention. One of the workmen was straining to reach a lantern that was hanging askew, and was leaning way past the railing on the metal scaffolding. She shuddered. That was definitely not a job for the faint of heart. Evie was not a fan of superhigh places. Darbs had talked her into going on one of those drop towers and had said it wasn't as high as it looked from the ground. But it was. It was every bit as high. Once she'd gotten to the top, she'd been pretty sure she wasn't going to survive the plunge to the ground. She expected her heart to give out halfway down. It hadn't given out. But she had given Darby a piece of her mind. One look at her face must have told her something, because her friend had stopped laughing and hugged her instead. "I'm sorry, Evie," she'd said. "I didn't think you would be that scared."

But she had been. Almost as scared as she'd been when Darby had shown her those pictures of Brad and she'd realized that her life was about to radically change. The last year had been harder than she ever could have imagined, and while the betrayal had eroded her confidence in her ability to judge character, it had also caused her to grow stronger and more independent. And it looked like she and Max were on their way to mending their friendship.

A silver lining, for sure. Only time would tell if it would last.

One of the hotel's staff came into the room and headed their way. "Do you have any questions? Or any special requests?"

Evie shook her head. "I can't think of anything at the moment." She glanced at Max, who shook his head.

"Well, if you do, please feel free to get in touch with me." The woman handed her a card.

"I will, thank you."

She left and Evie sighed. "Can you think of anything else we need to see?"

"Not off the top of my head, but then again, I haven't been to one of these events."

She grinned up at him. "Well, that's all about to change."

"I guess so." There was a pause and then he added, "Speaking of events, would you be interested in—"

Just then, she heard a shout from above her and glanced up just in time to see the scaffolding tilting to the side. The man who'd been leaning quickly moved back to the middle, but it did nothing to right the structure. Instead, like something out of a movie, it continued to tilt farther and farther, gaining speed as the legs on that side collapsed inward. Two of the men were clinging to the side boards, but one of them slid down the side and hit the ground with a loud thunk and lay there unmoving. Max hurried over to him, and as the same employee who'd talked to them a few minutes ago appeared in the doorway, Evie yelled, "Call 911!"

A cell phone appeared in the person's hand and she assumed she was calling for help.

Max was near the collapsed side of the structure, taking vitals, but when Evie glanced at the scaffolding, she realized if it fell farther, or boards started to rain down, they were going to land right on Max and the victim. And if those men holding on for their lives couldn't maintain their grip, they were going to have two more injuries, or worse.

"Hold on!" she yelled up to them. "Help is on the way."

At least she hoped it was. She made her way to Max.

"We need to move him. That thing could collapse completely and come down on both of you."

"His leg's broken at the very least, and I'm thinking he has head trauma. One of his pupils is blown."

She knew the dangers of moving someone

with unknown injuries, but if the scaffolding continued to fail...

The sound of something mechanical caught her attention and she saw a small skid loader being driven into the room. The driver moved the vehicle to the collapsed side of the scaffolding and raised the mechanism so that it bolstered the structure. Smart. Maybe that would help hold it in place until help could arrive.

As if summoned out of thin air, two firefighters appeared in the doorway and immediately entered the room and assessed the situation. One of them nodded at the forklift operator. "Thanks."

Max continued to monitor the downed man as they waited for the EMTs to arrive.

The other firefighter moved to the far side of the scaffolding and called up, "Are you injured?"

Both of the men stated that they were okay.

"Is it safe to try to climb down?" one asked. "We don't want it to completely collapse."

"If you feel you can. If not, we have some harnesses being unloaded even as we speak."

One of the men swung his legs over the side and picked his way down diagonally. The second soon followed his lead, taking the very same path.

Evie held her breath as they continued down, but they both seemed sure about the placement of their hands and feet. When the first one got to the firefighter who'd spoken to them, he allowed himself to be helped onto the ground, where he sat down in a rush. The second firefighter had him put his head between his knees. Evie hurried over to them.

"How is he?" she asked the firefighter.

"Honestly? He's extremely lucky."

Squatting next to him, she took his pulse as the other man was helped off the structure.

Then the place was suddenly teeming with police and EMTs, who rushed in with their bags and each went to a different victim. But the men who climbed down were found to be in perfect condition, except for having the living daylights scared out of them. And this was nothing like the drop tower, because while Evie had been scared out of her mind, the rational side of her knew that she was in no real danger. These men, however? They'd known very well that they could die at any given moment. It gave her a hard dose of reality. In all her years of practicing medicine, that whole scenario of "is there a doctor in the house?" had never happened to her. Until now.

She asked one of the emergency services guys, "Which hospital are you taking them to?"

"Vegas Memorial."

Their hospital. "That's great. We're both doctors there."

"I thought I recognized you, although we normally deal more with the ER crew. Looks like it was lucky you were here when it happened."

She glanced at where Max had handed off his patient to another paramedic. She was glad she didn't have to do what these guys did on a regular basis. She was sure if she'd had to climb that scaffolding, she would have. But she was so, so thankful that it hadn't come to that.

She nodded at the forklift driver, who looked like he couldn't have been older than nineteen or twenty. "We were lucky that hotel staff member thought quickly and brought in the skid loader. He may have saved those two men from having the whole structure collapse."

"Agreed."

The EMT guy went over to speak to the man who was leaning against the wall, looking a little pale himself. He shook his hand and patted him on the back. It made Evie smile. She was glad he'd received a little recognition for his act. She doubted he would forget this moment. At least not for a very long time.

She knew she wouldn't, either.

She went back to stand by Max, and nudged him with her shoulder. "You okay?"

"Yes. I'm happy as hell we didn't have to make the decision to move him." The EMTs had stabilized the man's neck and slid a backboard under him.

"They're taking him to our hospital, so we should be able to check in and see how he's doing."

Max's phone pinged and he got it out to look at it. A second later, his lips twisted. "It's Margaret Collins. She's asking to go home."

Her heart cramped. She understood where the woman was coming from. If Evie thought she was going to die, she wouldn't want to be in a hospital, either. She'd want to go home to her own bed. "She can't. Not yet."

"No. That chest tube has to stay in for the next day or so. I need to go."

"I'll come with you. I think we've done everything we can here." Besides, she wanted to ask him what he'd been about to say to her before the scaffolding collapsed. Something about an event she might be interested in?

A police officer came over and asked if he

could take a statement from one of them. She guessed she'd have to ask him later. Looking at Max, she said, "You go on. I'll stay here and talk to him."

"You sure?"

"Yes. Tell Margaret that I'll be there to see her in a little while."

"Will do. See you back at the hospital."

As she watched Max's strong back retreat through a doorway, she closed her eyes for a second. That had been so scary. And the thought of that heavy support structure collapsing on top of Max and the victim had rippled through her head and filled her with fear.

It would have been the same if had been Darby.

No, it wouldn't. She loved her friends dearly and would never choose one's life over the other's. But the thought of Max being severely injured or dying hit a visceral spot inside of her.

One that she knew existed, but that she tried to keep buried and out of sight. It was the same one that had held a tiny hope when he'd kissed her all those years ago only to have it snuffed out in an instant.

The police officer asked her a question and she shook off her thoughts and tried to concentrate on what he was saying, thankful for the distraction.

But what was going to happen when the distractions were all gone and she had time to think?

She didn't know. But she'd better figure it out before that happened, or she was going to get herself into a situation she didn't want to be in. And she had no doubt that Max wouldn't want her to be there, either. Because it would mean that she cared about him a little too much and in the wrong way, and that would not be good. For either of them.

CHAPTER SIX

EVIE ARRIVED JUST as he was getting ready to leave Margaret's room. He had talked her into staying until the drain tube came out, but just barely. She was in pain, which was understandable given the procedure she'd had. But it was also her breathing. She feared she was having an asthma attack and the nurse had refused to give her an inhaler without Max's permission. The nurse had evidently called when he'd been in the throes of helping their scaffolding victim, and he'd missed it. He couldn't imagine how scary it must have been to have had her meds withheld. But it wasn't the nurse's fault, either—she'd been following what the chart had said, and Max had wanted either he or Evie to check on her if her breathing problems got worse. And neither of them had been there.

But once he'd gotten to the hospital and had okayed a breathing treatment, Margaret felt a little better. But it was as if she knew her days were numbered and didn't want to spend the remainder of them in the hospital, despite the fact that both of her children were there with her.

He sat with her and shared that he wanted to get a PET scan and that would give them some more information. It was a tricky balance of not giving the family false hope, but also not bringing down doom and gloom before they knew what they were facing. He might "think" he knew, but until he had the evidence to prove it, he tried to always err on the side of hope. At least whenever it was possible.

He paused just outside the doorway to share with Evie what had been said. When he finished, she nodded. "I would have done the same. I'll go in and visit with her and if she asks I'll reaffirm what you just said."

"Thanks. I'm going to see if our scaffolding guy has arrived yet. Do you want to be updated?"

She glanced at him as if in surprise. "Of course."

"Alright. I'll give you a call once I hear something."

"Sounds good. Thanks." She stopped him before he could leave with a hand on his arm. "Wait. What were you going to say to me at the hotel? Something about some event?"

Damn. In the chaos, he'd totally forgotten about the two tickets he'd bought for the musical. And the doubts he'd had about them going together had seemed to grow the more time that passed. "It was nothing."

"No, seriously. I want to know."

He shifted from one foot to the other. "I actually have two tickets to the musical you wanted to go to. And was wondering—as an olive branch for some of my less intelligent moments over the last couple of years—if you might like to go to it."

Her eyes widened. "Are you serious? You really want to go?"

"Why wouldn't I?" Actually he could think of a hundred reasons why it might not be such a good idea. But now that the words had been tossed into the universe, there was no way he could retract them.

"I wasn't sure if satire was your thing."

"If you decide to go with me, I guess we'll find out."

She laughed. "Well, in that case, I absolutely want to go. When is it?"

That was something he hadn't even given thought to. What if she had to work that night? He found himself hoping they could somehow make it work. "Next Tuesday night at eight."

"Really? That's perfect because I get off at five that night. It'll give me time to go home and change."

Her eyes were sparkling and he was suddenly glad he'd asked her. It made her happy to go, and that made him happy. And he wasn't sure why, other than what he'd said, which had been the truth. He did see it as a way of making up for being an absentee friend. He just hoped it didn't backfire on him. "Well, then that works out for both of us. Talk to you in a little while."

With that, he left the room and headed down to the emergency room, glancing at the courtyard as he crossed the atrium on the ground floor. The sun was out in full force and the sidewalk outside looked dry and parched, a sign that there still hadn't been a drop of rain in almost two months. It was good that what Evie liked to call the "after party" of the gala wouldn't begin at the hospital until after the sun had gone down and things had cooled off.

There would be no mist machines set up or temporary fountains or anything that involved water, since there was no end in sight to the restrictions that had been set in place. Nothing but a good long rain would remedy any of that. Even an ice sculpture, although not forbidden, would probably be frowned on by some of their benefactors. Evie hadn't wanted anything that could be seen as wasting that precious resource.

When he glanced at the large television as he passed by, there was a report talking about the rain levels being much lower than normal, even for Nevada. They were hovering near the lowest recorded rainfall in the history of the state. The people in Las Vegas who'd opted to try to maintain lawns had found that even the smallest patches had turned brown. Some had decided to rip them up and turn to xeriscape landscaping instead, which had always been popular in desert climates. The hospital had been one of those places that had recently changed landscaping companies to focus on water conservation.

He sighed and kept moving. He'd been born and raised in Las Vegas and had never thought of moving, but sometimes the reality of living here could be frustrating with the constant traffic and how busy the strip could be, but it was also full of life and laughter, and people who exited the shows and casinos smiling. Those chapels of love were also a big draw for the area, probably producing some of the shortest-lived marriages in the history of the US, but even those were fun and light. His parents had been married in one of those chapels, but theirs was one that had endured, at least until his mom's death had cut it short.

And why was he thinking of any of that? Their marriage wasn't one of the happy-ever-after stories from the pages of a storybook. And yet, they had been happy. At least until his mom's diagnosis.

Thankfully, the emergency room was bustling with activity and pulled him from his thoughts. He went over to the nurse's desk. "Any idea where the man injured in a scaffolding accident is?"

The nurse glanced at a computer screen. "He's actually in room one. Dr. Wilson is with him."

"Thanks." That was a good call. Todd Wilson was the head of neurology and a great doctor.

He headed over to the room and gave a quick knock before entering. Todd was leaning over the patient, whose eyes were actually open. The neurologist glanced his way. "Ah, Max. I hear you played hero today."

"No, Evie Milagre and I just happened to be in the right place at the right time."

He smiled. "That's not how I hear it. Grady

here was just telling me that the rest of that scaffolding could have come down at any time."

Max moved closer. How had the patient even known that? He'd been unconscious at the time. He looked down at the man. "Glad to see you're awake. How are you feeling?"

"I have a massive headache." Grady's voice was rough-edged, probably from pain.

"I'm not surprised. That was quite some fall." Max glanced at his colleague with an unspoken question in his eyes.

"He's pretty lucky. He's got a big knot on the back of his head, and we're going to send him for a CT scan to make sure I'm not missing anything, but I think he's going to be okay."

"Thanks to you, Doc." Grady forced a smile. "Where's your lady friend? I'd like to thank her as well."

Oh, hell. Thank heavens Evie wasn't here to hear that. "She's actually a doctor here at the hospital as well."

"Oh, I thought you were at the hotel looking to see if it would work for your wedding reception. Sorry."

Todd's eyes twinkled. "Wedding reception, eh? Is there something I should know about?"

The neurologist no doubt knew exactly why

he and Evie had been at the hotel. "You know my philosophy on marriage."

"Actually, I don't. Care to enlighten us?" He winked at the patient, who smiled.

"Not really. Suffice it to say I won't be visiting any of the area's wedding chapels anytime in the foreseeable future."

Just at that moment, Evie poked her head in the door. Great. This was all he needed. To have this little joke expanded on and dissected.

"I thought I'd come and check on him myself," Evie said. She came into the room. "I'm glad to see you're awake."

He nodded. "I'm glad to wake up and find I'm not sitting on a cloud playing a harp."

He was right. That scaffolding was heavy. If one of the pipes had broken free and landed on him, things might have turned out very differently. But it looked like this was one story that might have a happy ending. He was sure Todd saw his share of tragic outcomes himself, given the line of work he was in.

Evie came closer. "I'm glad you're not, either."

"So you're a doctor, too?"

"Yep. Evie Milagre, nice to meet you. I was there at the hotel as well. Dr. Hunt and I were looking at the venue for the hospital's gala."

Although it was normal to use titles in front of patients, it always seemed weird when Evie referred to him as anything other than Max. Or Maximilian, if she was feeling playful.

The man nodded before wincing. "I thought you were there for a different reason, but Dr. Hunt set us straight pretty quickly."

Her head tilted sideways, and Todd said, "He thought you and Dr. Hunt were getting hitched. Max jumped right on that and assured us that wasn't the case, nor would it ever be the case."

A strange look went through her eyes before she masked it with a smile. He frowned. It had to be a figment of his imagination. After all, she'd married Brad, and other than that kiss in front of the venue where *Wicked* had been playing, there'd never been any indication that she had any interest in him as anything other than a friend.

Except, then there'd been that second kiss, too. That one had thrown him for an even bigger loop. Because he'd been about to let things go a whole lot further than they had. And Evie certainly hadn't seemed opposed to that happening, either. At least not from the way she kissed him. There'd been a slow thoroughness to the way her mouth had molded itself to his. To the way her fingers had tightened their grip on him—as if she never wanted to let him go. It had set him on fire and made it almost impossible to pull away. But he'd had to. For both of their sakes. Because what he'd wanted out of that encounter had been purely physical. And Evie? He had a feeling she wanted more. More than he could give.

Her smile held steady. "Dr. Hunt and I have been friends for a very long time. But we wouldn't last two seconds as a couple." She gave a quick laugh.

What was that supposed to mean, that they wouldn't last for two seconds?

"That's right. Evie is far too picky and controlling for me."

After a second of no response, she finally made a face at him. "And you are far too overbearing and ridiculous for me."

"Oh, really?"

Evie thought he was overbearing? That was kind of a punch to the gut. But was it any worse than him calling her picky and controlling?

No. So maybe she felt like it was just as mean-spirited. But he'd been joking, choosing words that didn't describe her at all. Because the ones that he would have chosen in real life were the ones that made her hard to resist. Even for an old friend.

But he did want to explain that he didn't see her as either of those things, he'd just been trying to be funny in a not-so-funny situation.

He moved closer to her, so that he could shake Grady's hand. "It's good to see you awake and in good spirits. Let's not have any more scaffolding accidents."

"Yeah, I think I'm going to keep both feet on the ground for the next couple of weeks."

"Good plan. Take care."

Grady nodded. "You, too, Doc. And thanks again."

"You're very welcome."

He went outside to wait for Evie, although he wasn't sure that was the best idea. Maybe he should just leave well enough alone. But he never wanted to hurt someone even unintentionally. And that look she'd given him…

A minute later, she came sailing through the door, throwing a comment behind her as it closed. Her eyes widened when she saw him there.

"Is something wrong? Margaret?"

There was something wrong, but this time it wasn't with Margaret.

"No, I just wanted to make sure you knew I was joking in there, earlier."

"Joking? About which part? About us never

being a couple?" She crinkled her nose as if to show him that she was not serious.

"No, about you being picky and controlling. I don't think you're either of those things. It was meant to be funny, but as soon as the words left my lips, I realized they could be construed as something that I really think. I don't."

She nodded, eyebrows going up. "I assume you want me to say that I don't think you're overbearing or ridiculous?"

"It would be nice."

And just like that, their relationship had shifted back over to the fun friendship they'd always had. Except for the last couple of years, when things had gotten so weird. He was suddenly glad he'd gotten those tickets and that he'd asked her to go with him.

"Sorry, Charley. No can do."

He laughed. "Why did I know you were going to say that?"

"Because, like I said to Grady, we've known each other a very long time. And I need to prep you for that musical we're going to see."

"Yes, you do." He paused. "I'm glad you can go."

This time there was no mirth in her smile, but there was a sincerity that came through in her eyes. She touched his arm. "So am I, Max. So am I."

He glanced at his watch, almost sorry that he was due to see a patient in a half hour. "Sorry to seem overbearing and ridiculous, but I need to go."

"Sorry to seem picky and controlling, but so do I. See you around, Max."

With that, she walked away, and damn if it wasn't hard to look away from the curve of her butt as she retreated. But he forced his eyes up and turned, then strode down the corridor at a pace he hoped would leave the mental image of his hands sliding over that shapely derrière behind.

She and Max had a dinner meeting scheduled with Arthur Robbins in a half hour to discuss where they were with the plans for the gala, which was coming up in just over a month. It was hard to believe that much time had passed since they'd agreed to work on it together. She had to admit, it had brought them closer and had seemed to iron out the creases of neglect that had plagued their friendship over the last couple of years. Three weeks ago, she'd never have imagined they'd be going to the theater together.

She'd even purchased two new dresses. A blue cocktail dress for the theater and a long black sequined affair for the gala that was off the shoulder, but had a detachable chiffon mini train in back that just scraped the floor. She would definitely be removing that for the courtyard portion of the gala, so that it didn't get snagged on the concrete walkway. It had been years since she'd bought anything for the galas. She normally just recycled some of her old formals for the events. But she found she just wanted something new this time. And she wasn't sure why.

She was nervous about the meeting. Maybe because the other two times she'd gone to see Dr. Robbins, he'd always seemed underwhelmed by the hard work they'd done on the gala, even when she'd gone to him with Max's sketch. Oh, he'd said he liked it and wanted it to happen, but there'd been no warmth in his voice to back up his words. Was he really that cold?

She also found his choice of restaurants a bit odd. A pancake house. For dinner. Somehow, she couldn't see the formal CEO eating a stack of strawberry pancakes, so this should be interesting. She and Max were going to meet outside the hospital and walk the two blocks to the restaurant. As soon as she got outside the building, though, she started having second thoughts. It was blistering hot, and most of that heat seemed to be emanating from the black-top. She was pretty sure her rubber-soled shoes were in danger of melting into the pavement.

She glanced around hoping to see Max so they could be on their way, when a car pulled up next to her. When the window rolled down, she realized it was the man in question. "Care for some air-conditioning?"

She closed her eyes in bliss as a hint of cool air drifted toward her from the open window. "Oh, God, yes, yes, yes!"

As soon as she opened the door and stepped into the chilly space, she realized her words could have come across as orgasmic. She let out a laugh. It wouldn't be too far off the mark.

"What?" he asked.

She cast about for an explanation for her ridiculous laugh and came up with a quick response. "I was mentally moaning that it was too hot to walk, and here you came with your already cooled car. It was as if you could read my mind." Actually, she was pretty glad he couldn't because she would be mortified. Just like she was about choosing the word *moaning*. What if those were both Freudian slips?

Then she'd just have to make sure there were no more of those.

"I went out to the courtyard to kind of refresh my memory about the layout before the meeting and thought the same thing. That this heat is unbearable. It's why I don't jog during the day."

That's right. The man ran marathons. He'd dragged her to one of them years ago and she thought she was going to die. She'd been short of breath and had sweat buckets, even in the cool of the evening. "It's why I don't jog at any time. Day or night."

"You haven't given running a chance."

"Yeah? Well, it didn't give me much of a chance when I tried it that one time."

His mouth twisted, as if he was amused, then he pulled away from the curb. "I should have insisted we train together, then you would have been fine."

Train together? She was pretty sure that wouldn't have gone any better. Because she would have just stared at his legs and physique, and probably ended up tripping over something and winding up on the ground in an ungraceful heap of sweatiness, which Max would never be able to unsee.

"I'm pretty sure I'm not cut out to run, training or not."

Maybe it was like Max, who'd once told her he wasn't cut out to be married. It was after he'd kissed her after the showing of *Wicked*. And it could have been construed from his reaction that she'd been looking for a proposal. She definitely had not. But she certainly hadn't expected him to overreact to the point that he made it seem that being with her in that way was the most hideous thing he could imagine. She'd been glad when he'd stayed away from her for a while. But then she'd missed him. And ended up regretting what had happened as much, or almost as much, as he'd seemed to.

But at least there was none of that today. In fact, over the last month they'd seemed to have drifted back into their old pattern of friendship. Margaret had gone home and at their appointment a few days ago, she'd seemed to be feeling better. She even acted like she was looking forward to starting treatments next week.

The PET scan had not revealed any lesions in her brain or liver, but had found one in her right breast and a mass in her lung. Chemo, while it wouldn't be curative, could help extend her life while maintaining the quality of it, hopefully for a few more years, depending on how the tumors reacted. But the hope was that they'd shrink enough that they could both be removed through surgery. The chance of recurrence was high, since the cells had already traveled once and were likely to again, but maybe they could keep that from happening for a long while.

He glanced her way. "Well, I certainly wouldn't recommend starting in the middle of the summer."

"Starting what?" Surely, he hadn't read her mind about Margaret.

"Running."

Oh! She'd forgotten that's what they'd been talking about. "I wouldn't recommend my starting it any time of the year. I'll stick to hiking. But you're right. Nothing seems very appealing when it's this hot. I wasn't looking forward to walking to the restaurant."

"Me, either. Speaking of which, we're here." He turned into the lot and they got out of the car and walked into the entrance of the restaurant.

"I wonder if he's here yet."

At that moment, Dr. Robbins came around the corner from the dining area. "I wasn't sure you saw me in there, so thought I'd come over and show you where our table was."

There were only three of them, but the CEO had evidently chosen a large corner booth at the very back of the restaurant. The table could have held double their number, but maybe it was just so they could have some privacy.

They sat down. Evie ended up sandwiched between Max and Dr. Robbins, which was kind of awkward. But at least the CEO was sitting on the other side of where the table formed an *L* so they weren't side by side. The former plastic surgeon intimidated her, for some reason. Then again, she'd heard rumblings from others that she wasn't alone in that feeling.

Just in case, she'd brought her spiral-bound notebook with all of the vendors' names and numbers and had hunted down pictures from last year's gala, since the decor was being done by the same company, who said they would make it almost identical to the previous gala. She figured it was better to play it safe, since having part of it at the hospital was already changing things up quite a bit.

He motioned for a member of the waitstaff. "I've already ordered."

Evie glanced down at her watch as surreptitiously as possible. They were still fifteen minutes early. How long ago had the man arrived? A tickle of dislike made the back of her throat itch. She cleared her throat to banish the sensation, trying to tell herself he wasn't trying to make them feel small and unimportant. But, trying or not, he was. And she didn't like it.

He waited until they'd ordered their meals before saying anything else. "Thanks for coming. I just wanted to see where we were and ask if there's anything you need me to do before the event. I collected the sign-up sheets and see a lot of our folks are planning on being at least here for the hospital portion of the gala."

Evie had wondered where those sheets had gone. One minute they'd been up, and yet when she went to gather them this morning, she'd found they were already gone. So he had her at a disadvantage, since she hadn't actually seen them yet. "I'm glad of that. Max and I went to see the venue last week and it looks like it'll be plenty big to handle the guest list. If I could look at those sign-up sheets, I would appreciate it, just so that I can get the final numbers to the caterer." The sheets had a place to check whether or not the staff members would attend both events—the hotel venue and the hospital—or just one, or neither. She was surprised Robbins wouldn't have realized that she would need them.

"Of course." He pulled out his briefcase and

handed her a sheaf of papers. "If I could get those back afterward, I would appreciate it."

That made her frown even as she promised that she would return them. What did he actually need them for? Was he going to keep track of attendance or something? If so, that rankled and the tickle grew stronger. Really, it was none of her business how he ran the hospital. But if he was going to treat the staff like preschoolers that would not go over well with the nurses' union or any other job representatives.

Their drinks came out and so did Dr. Robbins's meal. "Sorry, I have another meeting in an hour, do you mind if I start?"

When she hesitated, Max's leg pressed against hers, reminding her that she was the head of the committee. "Of course not, go ahead."

As he ate, she and Max shared what they'd gotten done from their prospective lists. And she was proud of both of them. They'd worked hard and had completed everything that could be done at this time. All that was really left to do was to finalize the numbers with the caterers and get a copy of Dr. Robbins's speech for the sound people in case he needed a teleprompter. But when she asked, he set down his fork and fixed her with a look. "I actually try not to give those out in advance, or at least not until the legal department takes a look at it. Just in case something gets leaked that shouldn't be."

Although he wasn't accusing her directly, it still bothered her that he would say something like that. They'd each done their jobs well and had given him reports without anyone fearing that something untoward would be done with those reports. But again, maybe something had happened in the past that made him leery of trusting anyone. But he would eventually have to trust his staff, or else he was going to find working at Vegas Memorial very uncomfortable.

"Will we be able to get a copy at all? The reason I'm asking is that we can have a teleprompter set up if you would like one."

Their last CEO had treated the staff more like family, and most of those people were still here. If the atmosphere changed too drastically, she could picture a mass exodus, making the hospital a shell of what it had been under Morgan Howard's term. She wondered if Morgan was keeping up with the goings-on at the hospital or if he was just content to go about his retirement with nary a thought about any potential problems crossing his mind. She kind of hoped it was the latter. She didn't think he'd like the direction things were now taking. In fact, she didn't, either. But she wasn't the one in charge.

Dr. Robbins finished his bite and then leveled another look at her. "No teleprompter needed. Do you need a copy other than for that?"

Max again pressed his knee to hers as if sensing her blood pressure was shooting through the roof. And it was. But he wasn't the only one who could keep a level head. She could be as civil as the next person.

"No. No need."

When he set down his napkin, she wondered if he had heard the undertones of her response without her being aware they were even there. But if so, he didn't mention it. "Well, I'm off to my next meeting. Thanks for all your work on the gala. The hospital thanks you and will pick up the tab for your meals."

Oh, you mean the meals in the place that you chose for this meeting?

But, of course, she didn't say that, just smiled and thanked him back, as did Max, who seemed a lot more sincere than her words had been.

Then he was gone, leaving his empty plate and a bad taste in Evie's mouth.

"What a dick." Her half-muttered words made Max laugh.

"Tell me what you really think."

She rolled her eyes at him. "I think Darby has the right idea about being her own boss. That's looking pretty attractive right now."

Their food came out and was placed in front of them, while the waitress whisked away Robbins's empty plates.

She glanced at Max. "Any thoughts?"

"None that I'd better voice aloud."

She relaxed, scooting away from him a bit so he had more room to eat, since the CEO was gone. His eyebrows went up, but he didn't say anything.

She thought he'd be glad to have a little more elbow room, so why did he look just the tiniest bit perturbed? But she wasn't going to ask. She was glad Darby wasn't here. That woman was an expert at cataloguing facial expressions and would have been sure to let her know what they meant.

She rolled her eyes even at the thought of having that conversation. But for all of Darby's quirks, they got along great—she was fun and loved to go out for a night on the town. Whereas Evie liked staying at home and relaxing, for the most part. But they balanced each other out and they were all for compromising.

It was one of the problems she and Brad had had, because he wasn't happy spending a lot of time just chilling with a glass of chardonnay and whatever show she happened to be binge-watching. And he didn't like compromising, so Evie had often forced herself to go out for a night on the town or to a casino with him, even when she was tired and grumpy after a long day at work. Instead of each giving and taking, she often found herself on the giving side, growing more and more resentful each time she gave in.

Maybe she'd contributed to him looking else-where, but if he'd been that unhappy with their relationship, he should have come to her and talked to her about it. But he hadn't. Instead he'd put in longer and longer hours "at the of-fice." One she'd come to discover he no longer had. And those long hours? Well, they hadn't really been about his job at all.

She shook off the thoughts. "So do you think we'll even get a copy of that speech?"

"I'm actually wondering if he's even writ-ten it yet. There's just something about the way he avoided the subject that struck me as more than being worried about leaks or the legal department."

"Well, that's just great. But why? This is his chance to show what a good leader he is and that he can be trusted with their donations. You'd think he'd be anxious to prepare for that. Instead he acts like he's more worried about how we're going to make *him* look."

Max shrugged. "We did our part. And since he couldn't think of anything to criticize or recommend, I'm going to assume he's happy with how things are set up. Now, it's up to him to be a voice the hospital can be proud of."

He'd said it well. And frankly, Evie *was* worried about what he was going to say. The reason past donors had given so freely was due to the warm and caring manner in which Howard conducted himself. If Dr. Robbins hoped to compete with that, he was going to need to step up his game and adopt some of that warmth. He might be an excellent administrator, but the jury was still out on whether or not he would be a good boss. She was surprised the hospital board hadn't pinned him down about what he was going to say. Or maybe he'd given them a copy and she and Max were the only ones he didn't trust with it.

Whatever it was, she could only hope things would go smoothly with the gala. All of it.

She pushed away her plate. "Well, I think that does it for me. Can you think of anything else that needs to be done?"

"Nope. Are you headed home or back to the hospital?"

"Home. I got off work a few minutes early to go to the meeting."

"Great. Do you have time to make a quick pit stop on the way back to the hospital, since your car is still there?"

"Sure? I'm assuming it's not a bathroom break since there's one here in the restaurant."

"Nope, not the bathroom. I'll tell you about it on the way."

CHAPTER SEVEN

MAX WANTED HER opinion on the playlist the DJ had sent him. But rather than just show her the list, he wanted to take her to hear some selections from it so she could get the flavor of the music. The songs would be piped throughout the courtyard, but the booth would be set up behind the temporary dance floor, so that people would feel free to dance or to sit around and watch as others danced the night away.

In the fifteen minutes that it took to get to his friend's little out-of-the-way studio, she didn't say much. Until they arrived and the sign out front proclaimed that this was where DJ Electric Nights was located.

"Oh! I've heard of him. *He's* the friend you were talking about? Why didn't you say so at the meeting?"

"Dr. Robbins isn't the only one who doesn't tell everything he knows. Besides, the guy is from New Jersey, so I doubt he even knows who Dale Night is, or would recognize his stage name."

"His name is Dale? I didn't know that. He always seems so mysterious with that mellow voice and those playlists he comes up with on his show. I can't believe you got him on such short notice."

DJ Electric Nights also had his own radio show, which made him one of the most sought-after DJs in Vegas. The right side of Max's mouth quirked up. "Fortunately, he had his vacation scheduled for that week, so he's just pushing it back one day for us."

"Oh, I feel bad that he's going to miss vacation time."

"Believe me, I'll owe him. Probably my football season tickets. He hasn't decided yet."

That made her laugh. "That hits you where it hurts."

"But it'll be worth it, won't it? Dale's worth it."

"Of that, I have no doubt." She leaned over and gave him a hug. "Thank you, Max. This means a lot to me. And to the hospital."

She pulled away just before his arms came up to go around her. An instinctive move, but one that he probably shouldn't act on. It was bad enough that he'd wanted to at all. And yet he did. Seeing the happiness on her face when she heard who his DJ friend was made things warm up inside of him.

"You're welcome. Shall we?" He motioned toward the studio.

"Oh, absolutely. Just kick me if I start salivating."

That made his jaw tense. He knew that Dale had this effect on a lot of the women who crossed his path, but somehow the thought of Evie being one of those women made him uneasy and he wasn't sure why. Maybe because she said she'd sworn off marriage and Dale was newly divorced, like she was.

That didn't mean anything. Lots of people got divorced. They didn't marry the next person that crossed their paths, though. Not that either of them were. Dale was also of the no-more-marriage camp. So even if Evie were taken with him, it wasn't likely to be reciprocated. At least he hoped not. Again, why it would even matter was beyond him.

Wasn't that the way he'd been about Brad? Except that Dale was a good guy, and Max had never had a good feeling about Evie's ex. Something that had turned out to be true.

And if she really did like Dale?

Then it was none of his business.

They got out of the car, and headed toward the door. Before they could get there, it flew open and a man bearing a slight resemblance to Jason Momoa stepped out. He wasn't as broad as Momoa, but his stage presence was every bit as striking as that of the actor. And Dale knew it and used that to good effect.

"Max! So good to see you." The man peered past his friend. "But who is this? Don't tell me you have a *girlfriend*?" His friend's eyes were trained on Evie with an interest that made Max tense further. He knew that look. It was on the tip of his tongue to lie and say that yes, he and Evie were involved. But then, he'd have a lot of explaining to do afterward. And that was one conversation he could do without.

"No. No girlfriend. But she is a friend. A *good* one." He tried to inject a subtle note of warning in there, but Dale had never been good at subtle. It was one of the things people found so endearing about him. "Dale Night, meet Eva Milagre."

Dale gave her a slow smile. "Oh, *miracle*. Very nice name. I think I'll call you my miracle girl."

Evie laughed, and it set Max's teeth on edge.

His friend went on. "You came at just the right time. I need *you*, Eva, to listen to a song from the playlist and tell me if I should include it. Or lose it."

"Oh, but I'm sure I don't know anything about playlists or how they're chosen."

"That makes you the perfect person to give me an opinion. I'll show you the ones I already have on the list. The one I'm on the fence about is very different as far as genre goes, but I think the message is perfect for the night." He pointed both of his thumbs at himself. "And *this* Night."

Evie actually giggled again, the sound light and magical. What wasn't magical was Dale calling her his miracle girl. He'd become somewhat of a serial dater since his divorce, but there wasn't much of a chance of him dating Evie. At least, Max hoped not. As far as he knew, she hadn't gone out with anyone since her divorce.

And if she chose Dale to be the first? Hell, what did he do if that happened?

Nothing. You sit back and let it happen.

Like he'd done with Brad?

Every time he'd seen Evie and her ex together, it had made a screw tighten in his gut. The sensation had grown so unbearable that he'd eventually stopped accepting invitations to things where he knew the pair would be.

Which meant that his and Evie's friendship had suffered. And in the end, she'd been hurt terribly by someone who was supposed to love her.

That same screw was beginning to turn inside of him. Why now? Just when they were starting to get back on track.

All he knew what that bringing her here might have been a huge miscalculation on his part. He'd hoped she'd be impressed, but this went way beyond that. But he couldn't very well rip her away and say they were leaving. Because she and Dale would both want an explanation for why he was acting that way, and he had none. Not even for himself, since he had no idea where this feeling was coming from. Or what it even was.

They went into the studio and neon lights surrounded them. They were one of DJ Electric Nights's gimmicks. He took a neon light to each gig he had, and whichever one he chose, it was the theme for the music of the evening. Whether it was Lovers in Peril or Love Overcomes or Lovers Inc. Every show he did had a calling card that was a play on words, just like the playlist he selected.

He pointed to one of the lights on the far wall and Max's fingers clenched at the words on it. It said Friends to Lovers with an artistic heart added after the words. Yeah, that was not going to be the theme of the gala, if Max could help it. But Dale was doing him a favor. And if he suddenly overruled the man on his lighting choice, he was going to ask why, and that wasn't something Max was going to admit to under threat of death. Although it was better than Strangers in the Night, right? Maybe, but not by much.

Max had fantasized once or twice about what it might be like to make love to Evie—okay, make that fifty or sixty times—but he wasn't willing to risk what they had on something that couldn't be permanent. It would be the same thing if he was fixated on Darby and acted on that fixation. Things between them would change. They would have to.

And if Dale and Evie spent the night together?

Not something he wanted to think about right now. Or pretty much ever. The last thing he wanted was for her to be hurt again.

Was that all it was?

He chanced a glance at her. She was gazing at his friend expectantly. *Ah, hell.* Why had he even mentioned having a friend who was a DJ?

"Isn't anyone wondering why I might have chosen that as the theme?"

"Theme?" Evie blinked as if coming back to awareness.

Dale laughed. "Okay, well, I'll tell you even if you aren't wondering. This is a fundraiser, right? Where you're hoping that people will be coaxed into donating for the good of the cause. *Right?*"

The emphasis on that last word told Max that his friend was waiting for a response.

He forced himself to answer. "Yes. That's the hope."

"Well, then all of those who aren't already involved with the hospital financially are friends who are basically coming to play dress-up and eat some great food. But the hope is that they'll go from being *friends* to being *lovers*. Let's call it a subliminal message."

Evie laughed. "Aren't those illegal?"

"All music at its heart, Miracle Girl, carries subliminal messages. Even orchestral music with no lyrics. Even the scores to movies. They're all meant to elicit an emotional response—in other words, they hope to move a listener to react in a certain way."

"True," she admitted.

"And *we* hope that listeners at this gala react by opening their pocketbooks and donate to something that gives back to the community in ways that go far beyond its exceptional health care."

Despite his uneasiness, that explanation made sense in a way that Max couldn't argue with. It had gone from a knee-jerk response about Max thinking about how it would be if he and Evie spent the night together, to seeing how carefully his friend had crafted a message for the event. He didn't realize how much work Dale put into these gigs.

As long as he didn't let his job venture into more personal territory.

As if waiting for something more, he turned to Max. "What do you think? Do you think it'll work?"

"I think it will. And we honestly need any help we can get this year."

Evie came over to stand beside him. "That we do."

They glanced at each other, and at her nod, Max saw that she'd had the same thought he had. That the new CEO was going to make it tough to get new sponsors. It actually made him relax a little bit. Maybe all of her attention hadn't been on Dale after all.

And if Dale could inject the warmth that Dr. Robbins lacked, maybe it wasn't going to be as much of a disaster as he'd feared.

"Well…" Dale spread his arms wide. "I'll give you any help I can muster. Now, let's look at the playlist and then I'll tell you about the outlier that's begging me to include it."

He put the list on the table and Max saw that it was a good mix of pop, rock and some lighter ballad-type songs. Most all of them dealt with love of some type. But then a lot of songs had love at the heart of their message. There were a couple of things that Max didn't recognize and Dale played those for them. One was a tearjerker ballad of regret and Max nodded, trying to see the choice through the eyes of the DJ. "The regret of not giving?"

"You got me, man. That's definitely the message for anyone who's hesitating."

Max put a hand on the man's shoulder, relaxing even more. "I've got to hand it to you. There's a reason you're the best in Vegas."

The man's head went back as if shocked by the words. "Just Vegas?"

That made Max laugh. "A little humility might do you some good."

"How about you, Miracle Girl, do you think I'm lacking in that department?"

Max noticed she hadn't said very much, but had instead listened to Dale give his spiel. That

Miracle Girl thing bothered him, though. And he wasn't sure why.

"Do you want my honest opinion?"

"I do."

Max would have expected Dale to look a little less confident, but if anything, he had a half-expectant smile on his face. One that he kind of wished he could wipe off. All he could hope for was that Evie was going to knock him down a peg or two.

"I think you're kind of a genius."

Max could feel his eyebrows crunch together, even while the DJ's arms spread wide again.

Far from knocking him down to size, she'd just added to the man's overinflated ego.

"And there it is. Humility, huh?" Dale said. "She can see where I'm going, even if you, my friend, can't. But you will. When you see those dollars pouring in."

What if she really did start dating the man? How would he feel then?

He groaned internally. He felt just like he had when she'd started dating Brad. All he could hope was that it didn't happen. And so he wanted her to be alone? No. But he also knew that Dale wasn't going to give her what she needed. Especially not after what Brad did to her.

"Well, I hope you're right about those dollars." He glanced at Evie. "Are you about ready?"

He hadn't meant to add that last part, it had somehow just slipped out. But now, Evie and Dale were both looking at him like he had two heads. Maybe he did. And one of them was taking exception to what was happening in this room.

He finally put a name to the feeling that was jabbing him in the gut. Jealousy.

Oh, hell to the no.

That's not what it was. It couldn't be, because that would mean…

It would mean nothing. And it would *change* nothing. Max didn't want a relationship. Not even with Evie. No…*especially* not with Evie. He wanted their friendship to go on exactly like it had over the last few weeks and in the years before her marriage. It had been fun and easy, at least for the most part. He was just being protective of her, that was all.

By admiring her body when she moved, or hoping she'd throw a little extra attention his way?

Like she was at Dale?

No. He wasn't hoping for that. Because—again—he didn't want a relationship.

"I still haven't played the outlier," Dale said.

Right now, the only outlier Max saw was himself. And he really didn't want to be played. Not by Dale. And not by Evie.

"What is it?" Evie asked.

He handed her a piece of paper. "You two read it. And tell me if the lyrics fit the situation or not. Then I'll explain my dilemma."

Max started reading and every muscle in stomach that wasn't already knotted went tight. The song talked about being let down so many times before. About being tired of getting hurt. About being tired of searching for answers.

The words could have been lifted straight out of his childhood. About his mom's death and his dad's descent into alcoholism. And his own pain and the hopeless anger he'd felt. And at the heart of it, the inability to change any of what had happened.

And then the chorus kicked in about someone special walking into the singer's life and how it had made a change for the good and how the person had transformed his life. It ended with saying she was his best friend.

He swallowed hard, and the jealousy he'd been feeling toward Dale seemed to fade away.

Because right now, he had bigger concerns. Namely, not seeing himself and Evie in those lyrics. They were just words written by some writer and sung by a random artist. He couldn't even put a tune to the words as he didn't know if he'd ever heard the song before.

Evie glanced up. "Wow. I know this song. And it *has* to be included."

"Ah…okay, Miracle Girl. Tell me why."

"I just think a lot of people will be able to relate to the message. I mean how many of us have been let down by people we care about? I know I have."

He swallowed. She had been. And not just by Brad. Max had let her down as well.

Her soft voice went on. "But then along comes someone who makes us believe that not everyone is like that." She shrugged. "Can't it be said of corporations as well? That we've all been let down by a business or other entity. But then along comes one that goes above and beyond and makes us believe that there's goodness in the world after all. That not every person and business is out for themselves."

Max nodded. He could see her point, and it sounded exactly like what Dale had talked about. How he wanted to make people believe that they were doing the right thing by giving to the hospital. And they would be. They could help more folks who, for some reason or other, couldn't afford medical care.

Dale smiled, a very broad smile that said Evie had given him exactly what he'd wanted to hear. "And that is why I wanted your opinion and exactly what my dilemma is. You say you know this song. What genre is it?"

Evie didn't hesitate. "Country and western."

"Yes! So will it sound off for it to be mixed in with all the others?"

She seemed to think for a minute. "I think the singer is well enough known that a lot of people will recognize it. I'm sure the song has been played at countless weddings at these little chapels around here. It's not an outlier."

Dale steepled his fingers and regarded her, and then he went over to his computer and tapped some keys, before stepping away. The sound of a printer starting up made Max turn to look at a long shelf where several machines were set up. A piece of paper came spitting out of one of those machines, then a second sheet, then a third. Dale went over and collected the pages.

"One for my friend Max. One for me. And one for my Miracle Girl, who gets me."

Evie smiled. "Glad I could help."

Yeah, Max was glad she'd been able to help, too, but if he heard the term Miracle Girl one more time he was going to tell the DJ exactly what he thought of him.

No, he wouldn't. Because for one, he liked Dale. The man had a good heart. Plus, if he said anything, Evie would want to know what was going on with him. And he did agree with them both about including the song. At least the business side of him did. The personal side of him said it was a very tricky business, which could get him into a lot of trouble. Because he knew himself well enough to know he was going to go home and play that song. And then it was going to wander around in his head until after this damn gala. And then, all he could hope was that he never heard it again.

But until then, he was stuck with it. And he had a feeling even if he objected to the tune being on the list, it was going to do no good. It was two against one, which made Max almost want to laugh. Because he didn't have to wonder long to realize that he really was the outlier in this mix. And he didn't like the way that made him feel. At all.

Max stopped in front of her apartment building and turned to smile at her. It was weird, because technically, the curving of his lips could be considered a smile, but it looked more like a pained grimace. In fact, he'd been strangely silent ever since they left his friend's house and she wasn't sure why.

She'd been wildly happy about what the DJ hoped to accomplish by letting his playlist get his message out. And she was pretty sure that every DJ gave an intro here and there to a specific song, or talked about the occasion, whether it was a wedding or birthday party or whatever. He would try to hammer home his message. And from everything she had witnessed, he was going to be successful at it. Who could resist that low sexy voice?

Her lips twisted. Actually, it looked like she could. He'd gotten her alone, while Max was looking at some equipment behind his desk, and asked her to go out with him. She'd had to tell him no, as gently as she could, and she wasn't sure why. Darby had been after her to get back into the dating scene, and Evie had been trying her best to start thinking in that direction. But when it actually came down to acting on her words, she'd chickened out.

DJ Electric Nights would have been the perfect person, because she had no doubt that he was a casual dater who went out with a lot of different women, sleeping with some of them and not sleeping with others. But there was no doubt that when a woman was out with him, he would make them feel like the most special girl in the world.

And God, she needed to feel that way. But she was scared to. And despite her words to Max a couple of weeks ago about not wanting to be in a relationship, the thought of going out with someone who would simply move on to the next person after their time together was done didn't sit as well with her as she'd hoped it would.

In fact, it didn't sit well at all. Maybe because that's exactly what Brad had done. Moved on to the next person. And she was pretty sure nothing was going to change her mind, which was why she should thank her lucky stars that the kiss she'd initiated with Max had been summarily rejected. What if it hadn't been? What if they'd slept together and he'd simply gone on, as if it had meant nothing to him?

She would be devastated.

Which is why she was not going to bed with him.

No, but she would be going to a musical with him in a few short days. What had made him get those tickets? Did he feel sorry for her?

She blinked back to awareness, realizing they were still sitting in front of her place and she'd made no move to get out. Did he think she was expecting a kiss?

Oh, God. She snapped open the mechanism that would allow her to get out of the car and practically fell to the ground in her haste to escape.

"Are you okay?"

"Of course. You?" She couldn't help throwing the question back at him, because he'd seemed to find too much pleasure in watching her try to roll gracefully from the passenger seat. She'd stuck the landing at least.

He turned to look at her. "Can I say something?"

"Sure." Although she wasn't sure she wanted to know what it was that he wanted her to do.

"Be careful around Dale. He dates a lot of women."

She blinked, trying to digest his words before the meaning hit her. "You don't think I can figure that out? I've seen articles about him. I know he's been divorced and that he dates a lot. But I'm not sure what business it is of yours."

"So you're going."

"What?" She stared at him. "What are you talking about?"

"I know he asked you out. When he mentioned the vinyl he had under his desk, I was pretty sure that was just a ruse."

She crossed her arms over her chest and bent down to peer inside the car, wanting to see his expression. "You're right. He did. What of it?"

"I just don't want to see you hurt." His low, gritty voice diffused some of the anger she felt over him acting like he could tell her what she should or shouldn't do.

"I'm not some fragile mouse who can't stick up for herself, Max. And for your information, I'm not going. I knew who he was the minute I met him. But that doesn't mean that I didn't enjoy him flirting with me."

"Flirting? Really?" The faux shock in his voice made a trickle of amusement go through her. "Flirting with Miracle Girl?"

She laughed, suddenly not offended anymore. Max wasn't just being nosey and giving her unwanted advice. He was concerned, and she appreciated that concern, even if it wasn't necessary. "I thought that was rather clever, didn't you?"

When Max didn't say anything, she climbed back into the car so she could face him on his level. "He didn't mean anything by it, Max. It's all part of his persona. I'm sure every person who steps into his studio is presented with the same one-dimensional caricature of his stage name."

"But you bought it. Told him you thought he was a genius."

"I wasn't lying about that. I do think he's a genius, when it comes to what he does—how meticulous he is about preparing for each job. But that doesn't mean I want to go out with him. Yes, it would be fun and exciting, but it could only be taken at face value. I think Dale has problems separating his stage presence from who he is outside of his job. And that's okay. It makes him happy. But when and if I ever decide to date again, I don't want it to be an act. Even though I'm not interested in marriage at this point in my life, I still want things to feel real and important to whoever I'm out with. I don't like games. I never have. So it's a lot, and not even I am sure of what I hope to get out of dating someone. After Brad it's…well, everything is jumbled in my head."

He linked his pinkie with hers for a second and squeezed before letting go. "You don't owe me any explanations. And I'm sorry for intruding. I just…" He shrugged, his voice dropping off in a way that touched her.

"It's okay. I know I don't owe you an explanation. I just didn't want you to think I'd been taken in by anything Dale said or did. Because I wasn't." She reached across and touched his face. "But thank you for being the good friend that you are. It means the world to me that you care enough to not want to see me hurt."

She wasn't prepared for the rough stubble that met her fingertips. It was earthy and real and made her shiver. Made her want to know what it would feel like in the morning after a long night of…

She pulled away, suddenly feeling shaky and uncertain. What had that been? That sudden awareness of him as a man, and not simply as a friend. She'd felt it before, but this was… She was not going to analyze it. She was just going to get out of the car and walk up to her apartment. While she still could. "Well, anyway, thank you."

She started to leave only to have him grab her hand and stop her, his eyes holding hers for a long minute before letting her go. "You're welcome, Evie. Have a good night."

"Y-you, too." With that, she got out and closed the door. With one more look through the window, she gave him a little wave and then walked away as fast as her shaky legs could carry her.

* * *

"That was so good, Max. Thank you for getting the tickets."

"You're welcome. It was fun."

They'd decided to go to Delacort's after the musical, and strolling down the street was reminiscent of the last time they'd gotten ice cream from the place. Only this time, both of them were dressed up. And when he'd seen Evie come to the door in that teal dress, his mouth had gone dry.

Dressing for the theater in Las Vegas meant just about anything went. Ranging from jeans to formalwear, people basically wore whatever they felt like. And her dress...

The dress was cut so that her shoulders were bare, and it clung to her curves in a way that turned heads—he found that he'd had trouble looking at where he was going. And yet, Evie seemed relaxed and happy and totally unaware of all of that. Maybe because of the show. The musical satire had been both witty and subtle, and the actors had truly been good at what they did.

Max had expected things between them to be a lot more stilted than they'd ended up being. When she'd touched him in the car a few days ago, he hadn't wanted her to get out.

He'd wanted to pull her close and hold her in his arms in a way that had nothing to do with friendship. And hell, he'd listened to that song that Dale had chosen for the gala and then had to play it again before turning it off with an irritated sigh.

"It's a shame that Darby isn't a big fan of live entertainment. I think she would have liked this."

Probably, he thought, but right now, Max was glad to have Evie to himself. Seeing her at Dale's had been a wake-up call. Someday she might find that special someone and they would lose their connection again. To hope that it might not happen was not only improbable, but also downright selfish. It would be the same if Darby started dating someone seriously. Most of her time and energy would go to whomever she was in love with. It was the way of the world. Except no matter how many times he told himself that was the case, he knew deep down it wasn't. It had been different when Evie had gotten together with Brad. She hadn't been the one to leave the friendship. Max had. Maybe if he hadn't, he could have spotted the danger signs before it was too late.

And that wasn't quite true, either. It was

more than that. But he couldn't quite decide how it was.

He was not in love with Evie. He could not let himself be in love with Evie. To go down that path would just bring so much heartache on both of them. He knew he had a problem with being intimately involved with anyone, but that trait had been seared into his conscience many years ago. He didn't know how to change, nor did he want to. He'd given his all to his dad. Had tried to protect him and be the emotional support he needed after his mom had died. And it hadn't worked. No matter how much he tried, it just hadn't been enough. Max had just ended up burned out and used up emotionally.

Evie's bare shoulder bumped his arm and he swallowed, realizing his ice cream was melting in his cup.

"What are you thinking about?" she asked.

He cast around for an answer, then said, "I wonder if Walter Grapevine was ever happy." Okay, it was stupid, but at least sticking to the topic of the musical was safe.

"I don't know. I think he just got so used to wallowing in the bad that he never opened himself up to opportunities that could have changed his life. Like when he had the chance to leave his job and go away with Tammy. He didn't. He chose to stay where he was."

This topic was safer? The musical hadn't had a happy ending, even though it couldn't be considered a tragedy, either. At least not from his perspective.

"Is that what you would have done? Give something up for love?"

"I think I tried to. With Brad. But I've learned there are no guarantees in life."

She took the last bite of her raspberry sorbet and dropped her napkin in a nearby trash receptacle. He did the same with his unfinished dessert.

"I've learned that, too."

She glanced at him. "Your mom."

"And my dad. He was completely lost without her."

"I remember you telling me that." She reached for his hand. "I think your dad was kind of a Walter Grapevine figure. He chose to stay in his unhappiness, never looking for anything beyond that."

"I know. But he was so sure there *was* nothing beyond that."

"Like I said, there are no guarantees in life. But it was his choice not to try, wasn't it?" They got to the parking garage and Evie let go of his hand. He immediately missed the connection. As they waited for the valet to bring Max's car, the topic changed yet again, and for that, he was grateful. Because Evie was right. His dad had made his choice and there'd been nothing anyone could do about it.

But hearing her say what he'd known in his heart to be true was somehow freeing. It took the burden off a kid who'd tried so hard to change things, but who couldn't. A ball of emotion rose up, threatening to overwhelm him. He glanced at Evie, and it was as if he was seeing her for the first time.

And yet, he wasn't. These temporary bursts of feeling for her had erupted from time to time over the course of their friendship. Usually when she'd had some sort of insight or tried to make him see hope in situations that seemed bereft of it. In a few days' time it would run its course. It always did. He just had to wait it out.

And if he couldn't? If he did something stupid and ruined everything? Then he was in for the biggest pity party in the history of man.

She might be Dale's Miracle Girl, but Max had to remember she wasn't his. Because there'd never been a big enough miracle to save him from what his past had made of him:

a man who, like Walter Grapevine—like his dad—was too afraid of pain and loss to let himself take a chance on love and everything it meant.

CHAPTER EIGHT

EVIE TOUCHED A finger to the picture Max had drawn for her years ago. It was in the entryway of her apartment, exactly where it had been when she'd been married to Brad. Her ex had never asked about it, maybe assuming she'd bought it at some out-of-the-way market. And he'd never seemed bothered by her friendship with Max, although Max had made it fairly clear that he and Brad would never be friends. And he'd pretty much stayed out of the picture during her marriage.

It was funny how Max had much the same reaction to his friend Dale's interest in her that he'd had when she'd been in the initial phases of her relationship with Brad.

Was that a coincidence or something more?

The musical had been so, so wonderful and sitting there next to Max had been...heady. It was the only word she could find to describe it. And it was totally different than when their little trio had gone and watched *Wicked*. Maybe because so much had happened since then. Evie had learned to treasure their friendship again. Was learning to be grateful for this new season in her life in a way that she hadn't been since her divorce from Brad.

She didn't want to be Walter Grapevine. She wanted to live. To enjoy life and friendship and lo— She stopped herself before she could go any further and ruin how lovely last night had been. Max hadn't kissed her when they stood there on the sidewalk in front of her apartment. But he had hugged her and thanked her for a wonderful evening. It had taken her a long time to get to sleep, despite the late hour, and she was still on kind of a high this morning.

She glanced at her watch. Ugh, she needed to get busy or she'd be late for work. After taking one last look at the picture, she headed to the bathroom to get ready.

When she arrived at the hospital, she was shocked to see workers out in the courtyard. She hadn't scheduled anything to be done until two weeks out from the gala, and they were still four weeks out at the point. Maybe Dr. Robbins had requested some repairs or something.

She met Max in the atrium to find he, too,

was looking out at the courtyard space, hands shoved into his pockets. "What's going on?" she asked.

"I have no idea. I thought maybe you knew."

"No clue." She blew a breath out. "I think maybe it's time I went to see our new CEO and see if he's behind this."

He glanced at her face. "Are you sure you want to do that?"

"You bet I am. It's one thing to refuse to let us have a copy of his speech. It's another thing to start interfering with our plans without even notifying us. I have workers scheduled to come in two weeks. I have no idea if these are the same ones, or if Robbins has gone out and gotten his own."

"I'll go with you."

"No, I can handle this on my own. Besides, if he fires me, he'll still need you to carry out his plans."

"No way," he said. "If he fires you, I'm gone, too."

That stopped her in her tracks, and she stared at him for a few seconds. "Don't do that, Max. People like Margaret Collins need you."

"They need you, too. If you haven't noticed, you're the first person she calls because you're the one she trusts the most. And I wouldn't have that any other way."

"I promise to *try* not to get myself fired. Does that help?"

"Yes. Let me know how it goes, okay?"

She bumped his shoulder, like she'd done last night. "I will." Looking up into his face, she stopped for a minute. The sun came through the window and cast a light on him that made him glow. He was gorgeous. Why had she never noticed that before? Well, she had, lots of times, but more in the sense of how one friend knew another one was good-looking. But this was a take-your-breath-away kind of response that only came with attraction. Maybe it was because of last night's outing. He'd looked incredible in his suit.

So what? She'd always been attracted to Max. Otherwise, those two kisses—one years ago, and one more recently—never would have happened. But she'd never let herself actually think about what they meant. Until last night and this morning. There'd been an intimacy between them during their trip to the musical that had stopped her cold, even without a single kiss.

Could she really afford to dwell on that, though? It had already gotten her hurt. Twice.

That picture in her foyer, as much as she loved it, only served as a reminder of one of those hurts. And yet, she could never bring herself to part with it. He'd made it. For her. And she loved it.

Just like she lov—

No! Do not even think it!

That half-formed thought from this morning threatened to break through yet again. And this time, there was no doubt about what it meant. She needed to get away from here.

"Okay—well, I'm off. I'll let you know how it goes."

He repeated her shoulder-bump move from a moment earlier and it sent another shiver of awareness through her.

"Good luck," he murmured.

"Thanks. I'm going to need it." In more ways than one.

Forcing her thoughts to something else, she went to Robbins's office and checked in with his assistant. Yes, he was in. And no, she wasn't sure if he was busy or not. But she would check.

Evie dropped into one of the chairs in his waiting room and wondered if he was even going to see her or not. If not, then what did she do from here? Just sit around and wonder if her workers were going to have anything to do when they arrived in two weeks?

Hell, she had no idea. But one thing she did know—she was not going to head up any more committees that Robbins had anything to do with. That included next year's gala. As much fun as she'd had with Max planning this one, she didn't think she was ready to sit in front of the CEO and watch him smugly inform her that she wasn't getting a copy of his speech. She hoped the board saw through the man before he did something that would hurt the hospital. He was either really, really smart, and would surprise the heck out of her, or he was a clueless narcissist who only wanted his own way in everything no matter what it did to anyone else.

Robbins came out of his office, and she stood to go shake his hand.

"What can I do for you, Evie?" Was it her imagination or was there a slight edge of irritation to his voice?

"There are some workers out in the courtyard, and I'm not really sure what they're doing. I don't have the preparations for the gala scheduled until two weeks from now. Does this have something to do with that work?"

"Ah, I see. No, this isn't for the gala. Not specifically, anyway. I just thought that maybe there needed to be another sculpture out there to go with the first one. It'll make more of a statement that way, don't you think?"

Except she'd only taken one sculpture into account when it came to the walkways. And if, as he'd said, it was going to be a statement piece, then it might change her plans for out there. "Is it going to be a big? Because that might mean we won't be able to fit as many people out there."

"Hmm, you yourself talked about having people in other areas of the hospital, did you not? So not everyone will be out there at one time."

That was technically true. But when she'd said that she hadn't meant that they could cram the courtyard with a bunch of new stuff, either. But to stand here and argue with him would accomplish nothing. And since he hadn't offered to show her a picture of the new addition, she was stuck. "Okay. I'll wait and see what goes in and then reconfigure the walkways to accommodate it."

"Good. That will work just fine then. Is there anything else?" He brushed his hands together as if he was already done with this conversation.

"I think that does it. Thank you."

With that, she turned to walk away, her jaw set into stiff angry lines to avoid telling the man exactly what he could do with his new sculpture. And God help him if the man erected a statue to himself. She might take a sledgehammer to the thing herself. Of course, she wouldn't, but it didn't hurt to at least pretend that she could.

Blowing out a breath, she suddenly felt a lot lighter. People weren't stupid. She had to believe the board of directors weren't blind, either. And since it wasn't just her who felt this way, others would catch on as well. Max felt the same way as she did.

She wasn't alone. And that was all that mattered. She had a feeling that things would work themselves out. One way or another.

The breathing treatment had an immediate effect on the young athlete, as the ragged coughing stopped, and she was finally able to take deeper breaths. The fourteen-year-old track star had wound up in the emergency room complaining of coughing and shortness of breath during training. There was no history of asthma, but Evie had seen this before.

"Did that help?"

"Yes. I feel so much better. I'm not sure what

happened." The girl took another deep breath and let it out with a sigh.

"Have you had this happen before?" She glanced at the girl's mom, who was seated beside her daughter.

"Sometimes at the end of a run, I feel extra tired. But today, I couldn't even finish the race."

Evie held up the spirometer for Delilah to try again now that she'd had a treatment. The girl took it and blew hard. Looking at the result, Evie smiled. "Much, much better than when you came to the hospital."

"So why is this happening?"

She took the instrument and put it on a tray to be sanitized, then came back and sat on a stool in front of the girl. "I think you're experiencing something called exercise-induced bronchoconstriction. It causes the airways to constrict, making it hard to breathe. It's similar to asthma. We actually see it in a lot of asthma patients."

Her mom spoke up. "Does this mean that Delilah has asthma?"

"It's kind of something in between. They used to call it cold-induced asthma, but obviously, we're in the middle of summer here in Nevada and it's not cold. But the thought now is that dry air is the real culprit, and since cold air holds less moisture..." She let her voice trail off before restarting. "We're in the middle of a drought, and although we live in a desert climate where it's almost always dry, there's even less moisture in the air right now. It dries the lining of the lungs and causes them to spasm when she's breathing hard."

"But why does it happen to me and not everyone?"

"We don't really know why it affects some people more than others."

"Does the mean I have to give up track?" Delilah's tone was one of devastation. "I love it so much."

"No, you absolutely don't have to. We're going to start you on an inhaler that you'll use before you start running. It'll help keep the airways open. A longer warm-up period before you start your practice may also help. If those two things don't do the trick, we have some other options we can try." She patted the girl on the shoulder. "The fact that you responded so quickly to the albuterol is a good sign."

Delilah broke into tears and hugged her mom before returning her attention to Evie. "I was so afraid you were going to tell me to quit running."

Evie smiled. "I'm not a runner, so I can't quite relate to the lure of it, but I know someone who is. And he would be pretty devastated if he had to stop, too. I know you guys are a dedicated crew. So keep on running. And I'll keep on doing my best to keep those airways open. Deal?"

"It's a deal."

She gave the girl's mom her card. "I'd like you to call and schedule an appointment so we can follow up on how things are going. Until then, I'll give you a prescription for the inhaler. If there are any questions, give me a call. My cell-phone number is on there."

"She has another meet the day after tomorrow, is it okay for her to go?"

"I'm going to say yes, but do the inhaler before you start and if you start feeling short of breath at all, stop. We may have to tweak things a bit, but I'm very hopeful."

The mom looked at the card. "Are you sure you don't mind if we call?"

"I'm sure." She didn't give her actual card out to all her patients, but this one was special, and she could tell that running was Delilah's passion. She'd told her the truth—she was going to do everything in her power to help keep that dream alive.

"Any other questions?"

Mom and daughter looked at each other. Then Delilah's mom said, "I don't think so. You'll give us a prescription for the inhaler?"

Evie nodded. "I will. Your breathing seems to be back to normal and the test we just did shows a vast improvement to how you were when you arrived at Vegas Memorial, so I think you're good to go. I'll get your discharge papers and prescription ready, and the nurse will be in to give you everything. And call and let me know how the track meet goes."

"We will."

Delilah jumped off the table, came over and hugged Evie tightly. She hugged the girl back, feeling a kindred spirit. Evie had had people in her corner helping her achieve her dream of becoming a doctor, and she'd vowed to do everything in her power to help other people fulfill their dreams.

She smiled down at the girl. "Take care and I look forward to hearing from you."

After Evie left the room and gave instructions to the front-desk attendant about the girl being discharged, and handed them a prescription, she headed to the elevator. It opened and she was surprised to see Max standing there. "Well, hi there. Fancy seeing you in a place like this." She was in a good mood that no one was going to ruin. Seeing Max just made that mood even better. "Not as fancy as Tuesday night. But then again, neither are you."

He grinned. "I'm crushed."

"Do you have a patient in the ER?"

"No. I was looking for you, actually."

Her heart sailed in her chest. "You were?"

It had been two days since she'd last seen him and the new sculpture in the courtyard had been installed yesterday. She wasn't quite sure what it was. It was oval-shaped and almost looked like some kind of tall obelisk. It stood side by side with the sculpture that was already out there, but the two pieces had nothing in common. But she'd taken measurements so that she could somehow maneuver the pathway between the two structures. It would be a tight squeeze, but there was nothing she could do about it at the moment, since it was obviously there to stay.

"Do you have any more patients?" Max asked.

"No, the one I just saw was actually my last for the day." He was acting a little odd. "Did you want to talk to me about something?"

"Yes, and it could affect the gala."

Her mood suddenly plummeted. "Oh, God,

what now? Is there a third sculpture going out in the courtyard?"

"No, but... Can we go somewhere outside of the hospital? I don't know if what I have to say is common knowledge yet."

Okay, those words were as obscure as the new sculpture. "We can. But I'm actually starving, so can we go someplace we can eat? I skipped lunch today."

It had been a crazy day with three emergency cases sprinkled in among her normally scheduled appointments. It had put her behind, so she'd worked right through her lunch break.

"Yep, how about that little Italian place we used to all go to?"

That "little Italian place" was actually a hole in the wall that the three of them ended up falling in love with. It held a lot of great memories of friendship and laughter. And, of course, since Max didn't drink, they had a built-in designated driver, which they always teased him about. But they both respected his reasons for abstaining and were careful not to overimbibe and bring back bad memories for him.

"I love that place. I actually haven't eaten there in ages. And right now, anything's better than the place we went to with Robbins."

"I don't think you're going have to worry about that anymore."

Her head cocked. "I don't understand. Did that restaurant get shut down?"

"Even better. I'll explain over dinner."

As soon as they got settled in the restaurant and she had a glass of wine in front of her, she prodded him. "So what's all this cloak-and-dagger stuff?"

"Cloak-and-dagger pretty much describes it."

She blinked. "Are you being serious right now? Did Darbs investigate someone other than my ex?"

"Huh?"

"Never mind. Tell me what it is."

Max settled back in his seat. "It seems all of us department heads were brought in for a meeting this afternoon with the board of directors and told that Dr. Robbins is no longer with the hospital, effective immediately. They don't want to make a public announcement at this point until they figure out how to proceed."

She stared at him, looking for any sign of humor in his face. Because if he was kidding right now, he was going to be in big trouble. "Tell me you're serious."

"I am. They looked for you when they called

us in, since you're in charge of the gala, but you were with your ER case and so they asked me to notify you."

She took a sip of her wine, trying to wrap her head around the fact that the man she'd tangled with about the new structure going up was no longer there. "How did this even happen?"

"His personal assistant went to the board with some concerns she had."

"And they fired the man based on that? And what about the gala? Will it be canceled?"

"No. It's going on as planned, including all of your ideas for using the courtyard for a type of after-party."

"Did Robbins even notify them of our plans?"

"He did, but he didn't tell them about a lot of other things, like his going to a couple of our donors and asking for a personal loan."

Shock held her speechless for a second. "What?"

"They evidently did a background check before hiring him, but missed the fact that the man has a gambling problem and there were some hefty private debts that don't show up on any credit reports. We weren't the only ones who noticed that he was behaving kind of oddly. Some sketchy characters came to his office not long ago when he wasn't there and freaked out Amanda, his personal assistant. That's when she started looking at what he did a little closer. The meeting he was in a hurry to get to when we were with him at the restaurant? Well, it ended up being with a loan shark who was calling in an overdue note, hence the phone call to the donors."

"God. I can't even believe this is happening. Who's going to be the keynote speaker at the gala?"

He leaned even closer, forearms braced on the table. "You're not going to believe this."

This time she laughed. "I pretty much don't believe anything you just told me."

He leaned back, putting his hand on his heart. "It's all true, I swear it. Anyway, the new speaker is going to be Morgan Howard. They're trying to coax him to come back at least until they can vet some other candidates. And do a more thorough job of it this time."

"I love Morgan. I don't begrudge him his retirement, but it'll be hard to fill his shoes. I just think they tried to rush things and didn't dig deep enough into Robbins's finances. I bet they don't make that mistake again."

"Let's hope not."

Their food came. She'd ordered the eggplant parmigiana and Max had chosen the rigatoni.

She couldn't help but smile. "Some things never change."

"What do you mean?"

"Isn't the rigatoni what you always got?"

"It is. And you liked the eggplant." He took a bite of his food. "And this is just the same as it always was. I'm glad the owners have always kept things simple, even though they're a lot more popular than they were seven or eight years ago, when we started coming."

"Me, too. And Darbs always liked the Caesar salad."

"With anchovies, of course."

She laughed, feeling inexplicably happy all of a sudden. "Those tiny fish always looked so sad lying on top of a bed of lettuce. I'll have to tell Darby the news. She's had to listen to me moan and grumble about gala stuff for the last few weeks."

She cut into her food and took a bite, as a thought hit her. Once she'd swallowed, she had to ask. "What are they going to do about that ugly thing in the courtyard that Robbins had commissioned?"

"The board didn't say, but I can't imagine them keeping it."

She blew out a breath. "This day has suddenly become perfect. I didn't have to kill a young girl's dreams and now the CEO from hell just got booted out of the hospital."

"Back it up a step. You didn't have to kill a young girl's dreams? Care to elaborate?"

"Just a patient I had today." She rubbed the back of her neck. "Some stories really do end well. And, as doctors, we need those, you know."

"Yes, we do. And then there was the man who fell from the scaffold. His story ended well, too, don't forget."

She sighed. "Yes, and in light of what could have happened, I'm grateful. It could have been so much worse. You could have ended up on the bottom of a pile of heavy metal along with our patient. And those other two men could have—"

"But none of that happened. It was a good day."

"Yes, it was." She thought for a second. "And so was today. First with the news from the board. And then eating at this restaurant again. It brings back so many good memories, doesn't it?"

"Yes, it does. Very good memories." His eyes locked with hers for a minute.

She couldn't stop herself from reaching over and catching his hand and giving it a soft squeeze. "Thanks for being there for me during the gala planning. And for the musical. You don't know how much either of those meant to me. It was like light at the end of what's been a long dark tunnel."

"I know I haven't been there for you during that, and I'm sorry. I know I went MIA during that whole thing with Brad. I kept feeling like I needed to somehow fix things, and yet, I knew I couldn't. And so I stayed away and let Darbs do the heavy lifting."

"I have no doubt if I'd have called, you'd have come."

He hesitated for a minute as if examining some deep part of his psyche. "Yes. If you'd have called, I would have come."

She let go of his hand and took the last sip of her wine. And that was enough sad talk for the night. "Hey, why don't you come over for some coffee. We can watch a movie or something. It's too early to go to sleep, but I don't really want to go out and do anything, either."

Again, he hesitated, and for a minute she thought he might refuse, saying he had something else he had to do. But then he smiled. "Sure, coffee and a movie sound good. And I'm not really in the mood to try to go out, either. How about if I run you back to the hospital and we can pick up your car."

"That sounds perfect." And just in case he was looking for an out, she added, "Don't feel obligated to come, though, if you'd rather just go home and decompress from the day."

The waitress came and handed them their bill. "Just pay at the front desk as you go out."

They waited for her to leave, and then Max said, "I do want to come. Sitting with someone who understands what a 'day in the life' is like is probably just what I need. I'm actually looking forward to the gala now."

"Even though it probably won't be a requirement for staff anymore now that Robbins is gone?"

He nodded. "In retrospect, I knew I should be attending it, but after so many years of sitting it out, it just became a habit. Kind of like Walter Grapevine. Maybe the nudge was a good thing."

"I think Robbins's method was more of a shove."

"Shove or nudge, I'm still going to go. Especially after seeing how much work goes into it."

She smiled. "And since DJ Electric Nights is our disc jockey for the evening?"

"It'll be good to see him do his thing. Just don't let him get too chummy."

"Define chummy." Before he could say anything, she laughed. "I'm kidding. You got your point across last time we talked about him. He's nice, though. I can see why women fall for his charm."

"But not you."

"Not me. Not after what happened with Brad."

"Good call." They paid their bill and headed out to the lot to get Max's car.

Once inside, it only took a couple of minutes until they were at the hospital and he was parked beside her car. "I'll lead the way."

"Sounds good."

With that, she got out of his car and jumped inside hers, then started it and backed it out of the spot. And then she turned it and headed toward home.

CHAPTER NINE

EVIE'S APARTMENT WASN'T far from the old one.
Maybe just a block away. She'd said that moving her things from the old place had been a
lot easier than she'd thought, since she'd left
all the furniture behind for Brad to take with
him. All she'd had to do was pack her clothing and her most precious possessions, and she
was out of there.

He pulled into a guest spot and turned off
the car, then joined her on the sidewalk. "I've
only seen your place from the outside. It's nice,
though. And I'm sure starting fresh was the
better option than staying where you were."

"It was really the only option, since Brad
had been out of work for a while and needed
the other place to be sold. But it worked out
for the best. This apartment doesn't have any
memories attached to it other than the ones I
put in it. And I tend to be pretty careful about
which ones I let in."

He could understand that. When his dad had died, his childhood home had automatically become his. It was paid off, and so he could have moved into it and saved himself some money, but the thought of doing so just made him queasy, so he'd sold the place. He'd donated the money to a well-known cancer-research place in honor of his mom.

Her apartment complex was a tall structure that curved partway around a pool, so that all of the units had at least one window that overlooked it, a great selling feature. They took the elevator up to the third floor.

"Very nice."

"It is nice. But it feels odd to have a big body of water sitting in the middle of the lot when the drought has caused so many changes in our personal usage. I mean, car washes are only allowed on a weekly basis and they've had to cut back on the amount of water per wash."

"Looks like they've saved water in other ways. Didn't there used to be lawn here?"

"There was. And they took it out. But I kind of like it. It's a nod to the reality of where we live, although it would probably be hard if the city were devoid of green spaces."

They stepped into her apartment, which was blissfully cool after the heat that had enveloped them outside. The marble floors probably felt wonderful on her bare feet when she padded around in the mornings.

And just like that, the image of Evie in a silky robe that was loosely belted around her waist came to mind, her nipples standing out in sharp relief against the thin fabric.

Hell, coming here had probably been a huge miscalculation on his part. Because he'd envisioned this as each of them watching a movie enveloped in their own little bubble of space. But when he glanced through the door into her living room, he saw that she had one couch and a chair—which he was certainly going to use. She didn't need to be sharing anything besides room space with her.

Just then, something hanging above the glass table in the foyer caught his eye. He stared at it for a second, realizing what it was. It was the picture he'd drawn her from *Wicked*. She'd taken the canvas and had it framed in black wood that looked ragged and bubbled along the edges, as if it had been in a fire. It was the perfect contrast for the pristine white of the canvas and the black inked images that seemed to jump off the page. He'd almost forgotten what it looked like after all these years.

"Wow. You kept it."

She glanced at where he was looking and gave a half shrug. "I really like it. And the fact that you drew it makes it that much more special."

"And the frame?"

"My dad actually made it, using a flame-thrower to blacken the surface and make it look older."

"It makes the black of Elphaba's robe stand out. I never would have thought to do that."

She smiled, touching the frame with light fingertips. "My dad can't draw, but he does have a great eye for putting the right frame with the right print. He did all of the frames in the apartment for me."

As he glanced back into the living room, he saw several other pictures each with a different type of framing material. Most were informal, made out of wood that was either painted or stained. As far as he could see, this was the only one made with a charred appearance. "I'll have to remember that. Does he do them for friends?"

"For you, I'm sure he would."

She tossed her keys in a wooden bowl on the hall table and motioned for him to come into the living room. He took one last look at the picture and followed her.

He wasn't sure how he felt about his work being given such a prominent place in her home. It created a warmth in his chest that could transform into a more dangerous heat given a little encouragement. Encouragement he didn't intend to give it.

So he turned his attention to the living room. Just like he'd seen from where he'd been standing, she only had a few pieces of furniture, including a TV stand with some drawers and another wooden bowl that held a couple of remote controls. She took one of them and turned on a ceiling fan that was suspended from a vaulted ceiling. He was glad because he was still a little warm—both from picturing her in a thin robe and from seeing how much care she'd taken in displaying his artwork.

She motioned him to the sofa, and so he gingerly sat on the long piece of furniture, hoping that she was going to sit in the chair adjacent to it. "Do you want some coffee or tea?"

"Coffee if you have it."

Maybe the coffee would help center him and keep him from falling asleep on her couch, something he did at home quite regularly. He'd kick his shoes off, stretch out on his long leather sofa and sleep an hour or two. But that was not something he was going to do here.

"I do. Black, right?"

"Yes, thanks." He tried to remember how she liked her coffee but came up blank.

When she came out with a tray that held a thick mug and a more dainty cup with the string from a tea bag dangling over the rim, he knew why. She liked tea rather than coffee. With her Brazilian heritage, he just assumed that coffee was a cultural norm. And yet, she had it in her house. For company?

"You don't drink coffee?"

She bit the corner of her lip. "Not a lot, but buying it is still a habit. Plus when I have company I serve it."

The way she said it was still a habit to buy it made him pause before he realized Brad had probably preferred coffee. Which explained why she always had it in the house.

He wished he could go back and change what had happened to her, but he couldn't any more than he could change what had happened to his mom. Or to his dad. Sometimes, it just had to be accepted that bad things happened and that there was no rhyme or reason for them. There wasn't necessarily a grand scheme that demanded they happen.

He tried to think of something to say about

coffee or tea, but came up blank, so instead he asked, "Do you use your pool a lot?"

"Almost never. When I'm home, I'm normally in for the night, and to change into a suit and go down there just seems like work. But most complexes have pools as part of the amenities, so I just go out on the balcony and sit and enjoy looking at it."

"May I?"

"Of course. There's a ceiling fan out there, too, and it's nice and private."

She followed him out to the balcony and unlocked the sliding glass door. Outside, she had a few potted plants, including rather healthy-looking tomato and pepper plants. There were small red tomatoes on the one bush, but nothing on the other. "Does your pepper not produce?"

"Oh, it does. They just never last because I eat them almost as soon as they're big enough."

There was a double glider swing on the side of the balcony and they settled on it together, thighs lightly touching. Maybe coming out here hadn't been such a good idea after all. He'd been worried about being too close in the living room. This was ten times more intimate. He set his mug on the table beside him and looked through the glass barricade that was the only thing standing between them and falling over the side of the building.

It was warm and dry, and there was no sign of grit on the tiled flooring from the dust storms that periodically rolled through the area, obstructing visibility and creating a mess. Part of the "blessing" of living in the desert.

"It's nice. My house doesn't have one of these. I'd probably be out here every evening." With the fan above them twirling and sending air over his skin, he stretched his legs out and glanced out over the empty pool area.

As if sensing his unspoken question, she said, "The pool normally gets busy after dinner, when the kids are out of school. An hour or so from now. It can get pretty loud."

"I can imagine."

"Are you okay if I go put some shorts on? It tends to be pretty warm out here."

"We can go back in, if you want."

She shook her head. "I like it out here. I just need something a little cooler. I'll be back in a minute."

As soon as she went in, he got up and looked over the balcony at the hardscape below. The sun glinted off the pool with enough force to make him squint. And yet he loved the desert, even during times like then when the heat be-

TINA BECKETT 203

came unbearable. Because once the sun went down, it almost always cooled down enough to open the windows and let some fresh air in.

Other than the *Walter Grapevine* production, he couldn't remember the last time he and Evie had gotten together and done something that didn't involve work or, more recently, the gala. Or that hadn't included Darby. To be here with her alone was…nice. It had a comfortable feeling, like wearing a favorite pair of jeans. Which made sense, since Evie was one of his favorite people.

She came back out a minute or two later and he turned from his spot to look at her. She had on black Lycra shorts that hugged her frame and made every curve of her hips and backside stand out. And she was wearing a white racerback tank top that showed off thin pink straps that were probably to her bra. The sight made him swallow.

A pink bra? The urge to trace his finger down the path of that strap on her back came with a strength that surprised him. When she leaned over the glass railing, making even more of that tanned skin visible, it became even harder to resist. Because he could just follow the path down, continuing its trajectory even past its boundaries, going over the small of her back until he reached the curve of her buttocks.

He swallowed and when her head suddenly turned and caught him staring, she blinked. "What?"

Hell, what could he say?

"I thought you weren't a runner?"

"Why do you say that?" She glanced down. "Ah, the outfit. Is there some kind of special runner's law that says no one else can wear spandex?"

"No. And it looks good on you."

Why he'd said that last bit was anyone's guess.

"Thanks. I'm normally out here alone. But once I get home from work, I'm ready for the clothes to come off."

"I guess you are." The image of that bathrobe came back to his mind and he wondered if she would lean over the railing just as easily when she was wearing just that. Wondered what it might be like to come up behind her and slide the hem of that robe up the backs of her thighs and...

She turned around and grinned. "That didn't come out quite right."

In a voice that sounded strangled, he said,

"I was pretty sure you didn't mean you come out here and dance in the nude."

"You know, when it's dark and the lights are completely off, it probably wouldn't matter if I did. No one could see." Her throaty chuckle did nothing to erase the image of her doing just that.

"Evie…" Did she even know what she was saying? How every picture she painted was being burned into his brain?

"What?" Her eyes widened as her gaze took a quick trip down his body, where he was pretty sure every one of his thoughts was there on full display. "Oh! I didn't realize that you… That what I…"

She bit her lip, then propped her hip on the glass barrier as she stared at him. "Would it really be that awful, Max?" Her words were so soft he'd barely heard them. But she'd said them all the same.

He could pretty much guarantee that whatever might happen between them wouldn't be awful at all. At least not on his end. But was it the smart thing to do?

Hell, did it really matter? She'd made choices she probably regretted and so had he. That didn't mean that this would necessarily be one of those choices, right? They'd kissed and their friendship hadn't gone up in flames.

But he knew something else that might go up in flames. Him. The moment that he touched her.

He should stop with those thoughts. Right now. But the note of uncertainty that he'd heard in her voice as she'd whispered those words had cut him to the core. So, reaching out, his hand encircled her wrist and tugged her closer. "No. It wouldn't be awful. And the way you're making me feel right now says it would be the opposite."

She took another step closer, until their bodies were touching. "Would it?"

Doing what he'd wanted to do just moments earlier, his free hand went to her shoulder and followed the hellish path of that bra strap until it disappeared under her stretchy shirt. He came back up and dipped his hand under the strap, loving the feel of the elastic across his skin as his thumb brushed against her soft skin. The sensation sent prickles across every nerve ending he possessed.

"Hell… I want to go back inside."

He could only hope she could guess why that was and that she was in full agreement with it.

"So do I. But I don't want to watch a movie. Not anymore."

"I was hoping you were going to say that."

With his fingers still around her wrist, he towed her behind him as he reentered the apartment and closed the glass door behind them. Then he turned her to face him. "Are you sure you're okay with this?"

"Yes. More than okay."

As if to emphasize that point, she stood up on tiptoe and kissed him, her lips soft and pliable against his. It only took a second for him to wrap an arm around her waist and fasten her to his body. Then his hand pushed deep into her hair and he kissed her in earnest, his tongue sliding along the seam of her lips until she opened to him. If she thought what she'd seen on the balcony had been obvious, then feeling the effect she had on him must be all the more apparent as he pushed his hips against her belly, loving the pressure along his length.

Except he wanted more than this. So much more. And this time he wasn't going to pull away with some glib speech about saving their friendship. Because if it could survive two kisses, surely it could survive sex. And it would be very good sex. It was in the way she whimpered against his mouth. In the way her mouth closed around his tongue and drove him wild with need.

He needed to find a horizontal surface. And soon. Or this was going to be over before it had even begun.

After pulling away long enough to mutter the word *bed*, he moved back in without waiting for a reply, his hand leaving her hair and traveling down the front of her body until he reached her left breast. It was perfection in his palm as he squeezed, finding her nipple in a millisecond.

"Bed." This time it was her voice repeating his earlier thought.

Oh, yeah, he'd wanted to find a bed. He'd almost forgotten. Scooping her up in his arms, he let her direct him to the first open door down a short hallway. Not bothering to shut it behind him, he entered the room and found the bed in the middle of the room. Instead of tossing her onto it and following her down, he turned his back to the mattress and lowered himself onto it. Lying back on the mattress, he took her with him. She quickly scrambled so that she was on top of him, the breast that he'd cupped now pressed tightly against his chest.

It was heaven on earth having her like this. Something he'd never in his wildest dreams ever pictured happening. But it was real. Evie was here with him, kissing him like there was no tomorrow. And maybe there wasn't. But right now he didn't care.

He cupped her bottom, pulling her tight against him and wishing she'd already shucked her clothing. But because she hadn't, he found the waistband of her shorts and pushed his hands beneath it and encountered smooth rounded flesh that sent his body into a frenzy of want and need.

"Evie." He pushed the clothing over her hips, and as if sensing what he was trying to do, she stood up and stripped them off her body, kicking free of them. His mouth watered. But when her hands went to the hem of her shirt, he sat up and stopped her. "Let me."

Pulling her onto his lap so that she straddled his thighs, he gently slid her shirt up her flat belly and over her breasts. When she held her arms high over her head so he could get it off her, he paused for a minute after he'd discarded the garment, one palm sliding up her arm and trapping her wrists in place so he could enjoy the decadent sight of her lacy bra against her skin, her breasts pushing tightly against it as if wanting to be free.

Soon. Very soon. But not before he did this.

Letting go of her wrists, he eased her forward until his mouth was against her breast. With it still encased in fabric, he found her nipple and used his teeth to grip it, wetting the lace and scrubbing his tongue across the sensitive part of her.

Evie moaned and pressed closer before she reached down and freed her breast from the cup and drew him back to it.

The sensation was incredible as he pulled hard against the nipple, her hands cupping his head and holding him in place. He finally couldn't take it anymore, so he undid her bra and tossed it across the room. Then he lay back as she remained where she was, her thighs on either side of his.

All that stood between them were his jeans and briefs. But first… He bucked up under her enough to slide his hand into his back pocket, then withdrew his wallet. He hoped to hell he had something in there. It had been a while.

Flipping it open, he found not one, but two condoms. Plans for how to use that second one were already forming inside of his head, but he put them aside for now, along with the second condom, barely able to reach her nightstand with his fingertips. The he used his teeth to rip open the packet he still held in his hand.

Before he could try to maneuver himself to where he could reach, she took the condom from his hand and went up on her knees. Setting it beside his hip, she made short work of undoing his button and fly and freeing him, her hand warm against his oversensitive skin. Her eyes came up and met his with a secretive smile as she pumped up and down with the perfect amount of pressure.

It was too much.

"God, Evie. Stop for a minute."

She did, halting her movements and reaching for the condom. She slowly unrolled it down his length while he muttered under his breath and tried to hang on to what little control he had left.

Her fingers drew circles across his abs, making his nerve endings crazy with the mixture of pleasure and ticklishness. He was so attuned to that that he completely missed her hips moving over him until she pressed down hard, taking him deep within her with a single movement. He swore out loud, gritting his teeth at the intense rush of pleasure that swept over him.

His fingers gripped her hips in an effort to slow down the wave that was starting to grow and gain strength. But she was relentless, as if needing something only he could give her.

The feeling was mutual. Because what he needed, only she could give.

And there was still that second condom…

Giving himself permission to just go with what was happening, he slid his fingers in between their bodies and found moist curls and that tiny sensitive nub that lay at the very heart of her.

She moaned as he stroked her with both his fingers and his body, using them both to bring her as much pleasure as she was bringing him.

"Max. Yes." Her movements quickened, taking him deeper with each strong pump of her hips. And the wave, which was traveling toward shore, grew to monstrous proportions, and he knew it would soon overtake him.

Just as it hit, she cried out, her hands gripping his shoulders and wildly driving herself onto him. Her body spasmed, once, twice, and then it contracted rhythmically around his flesh, finally forcing him over the edge. He saw white for several long seconds before he became aware of anything other than their frenzied movements and the ragged sound of their breathing.

She slowed the friction just before it became too much, her gripping hands easing their hold and smoothing over his chest.

That had been… More, much more than anything he'd experienced before.

When she finally came to a stop and sat atop him, her eyes landed on him as if seeing him for the first time. And it did something to him. Touched a part of him he wasn't sure he wanted exposed, so he put a hand in the middle of her back and eased her down until she was lying against him. But at least she could no longer see his eyes. Because what he'd seen in hers threatened to rock his world and topple everything he believed to be true.

But those thoughts could wait until tomorrow. When he would be seeing the world with more rational eyes. Until then, he could just lie here and enjoy the slight aftershocks that were still coursing through his body and making him jerk against her a few more times.

He was spent. Didn't want to move. Didn't want to think.

But he didn't really have to, did he? Not yet. He could just relax, revel in the release his body had just had and enjoy the feel of her body against his. Although the fact that he still had clothes on was starting to rob him of some of the joy of lying here with her. He could fix that later, too. But right now…

She wasn't moving and it took him a few

minutes to realize she was breathing in deep steady movements that made him smile. She was asleep.

And part of him was glad. Glad she hadn't tried to rationalize what had happened or try to talk through things. He didn't want any of that. He just wanted to be here with her.

If she'd been anyone else, he probably would have already been up and out of here. Or at least up and in the shower. He rarely took the time to wallow in the afterglow of sex. But this time was different, and it stole the part of him that sought to escape.

He didn't want to escape, because this was Evie and she was his…

Max didn't finish that thought because the word *friend* didn't seem to fit in this context.

Don't try. Just lie here and be with her.

So until she woke up, or morning arrived, whichever came first, he was going to do just that. Enjoy being with her.

CHAPTER TEN

THE SOUND OF something buzzing somewhere near his head woke him up. At first, he brushed his hand across his head as if chasing away a pesky insect. Then his eyes opened, and he wasn't sure where he was. Someone's leg was draped over his.

Evie. The events of the previous night rolled over him like a freight train.

They'd had sex.

He swallowed, all of the implications that he'd swatted away yesterday came rushing back. And this time he couldn't just ignore them.

He'd told himself that sex wouldn't affect their friendship, but now that it was staring at him in the cold light of day…

What was he going to do? He'd broken all of the promises he'd made to himself. Not about sex, because that had never been off the table.

But his rule was that he not be with someone that he was emotionally involved with.

Had he really broken that rule, though?

Hell yes. Because he was emotionally involved with Evie, he'd just refused to acknowledge it. So again, how was he going to fix this?

The buzzing started again and this time he realized it wasn't an insect. It was his phone. What time was it, anyway?

He reached for the item on the nightstand and felt the second condom, instead. It, too, filled him with foreboding. He'd had every intention of using it last night. Except he'd fallen asleep. Strike two for his promises.

Grabbing the phone, he sat up to answer it, and felt something on his shoulder. Lips. Very warm lips that trailed up his neck and sent a shudder through him. His eyes lighted on the condom again, and this time it didn't look quite so evil. Quite so nefarious.

He pressed answer on his phone in case it was something urgent and muttered, "'lo?"

"Max, is that you?"

He was awake in a flash when he recognized the voice of his personal assistant. "It is. What's going on?"

Evie stopped kissing him and came around the side to look at him. He held up a finger to signal he would be just a minute. And then what? Was he going to actually move on to round two with her?

The question swirled in his head as Sheila's voice came back to him. "Max, I have some news. Margaret Collins was scheduled for her first treatment today."

That's right. She was. He glanced at his watch. It was only eight in the morning. He wasn't due at the hospital for another hour. "She is, but that's later this afternoon, isn't it?"

"It *was*..."

Those two words came down like a hammer, shattering whatever had happened last night.

"What happened?"

"We're not sure. But her son went to wake her up this morning and found her unresponsive. She died in her sleep."

She died in her sleep.

The guilt that he'd not felt last night came pouring over him in a flood that wouldn't be stopped. His eyes burned and his throat went bone-dry. While he'd been rolling around in this bed with Evie, Margaret Collins had been taking her last breath. A sense of déjà vu went over him that wouldn't stop. She hadn't even made it to her first treatment.

Shades of his mom. Shades of people leaving

those they loved. Loved ones being left behind to somehow carry on.

It's not the same thing.

He knew that, but it still didn't stop his heart from trying to jackhammer its way out of his chest.

"Thanks for calling." It was all he could manage to get out before he hit the end button.

He was somehow able to get his feet under him and lever his way out of bed as a fog of regret settled over him, every bit as dark and heavy as the dust storms that ravaged this part of Nevada.

Then Evie was in front of him, wrapped in the bedsheet. "Max, what happened?"

"Margaret…died last night." He took her by the shoulders, even as he wanted to jerk away from her, the urge to escape beating through his skull. "I'm so sorry, Evie."

Her eyes closed and two tears escaped. "Did she suffer?"

"I don't think so. She passed in her sleep."

Brown eyes stared at him and a hurt almost as deep as when he'd learned his mom had died held him in a paralyzing grip.

He couldn't do this. Couldn't bear to see the devastation in her eyes over what had happened.

Margaret had been Evie's patient for years and so he understood those emotions. But what about the other ones? Like the fact that Margaret Collins had never gotten the chance to prepare? Had never been able to say goodbye to her family?

What if it had been him? Or Evie?

He didn't know. And things right now were so jumbled he couldn't make sense of anything. All he knew was that he couldn't stay here and think about any of that. It was why he'd been so adamant about not getting close to anyone.

And now, he'd gone and done the very thing he knew he shouldn't have. Gotten close in a way that had nothing to do with what they'd done last night.

He let go of her and closed his eyes, hoping he could do what he needed to do. "Evie, I'm sorry. Really, really sorry about Margaret. But I just can't be here right now."

Grabbing his clothes from the floor and pulling them on with a frenzy that came out of nowhere, he tried to put his thoughts on hold. Only they wouldn't go away, and kept swirling inside of him.

"Max, stop a minute."

"I need to get to the office."

"No, you don't." She moved in front of him

and threaded her fingers through his. "Please. Talk to me."

"Not now. Maybe later. I just need time to process this."

"Process what? Margaret's passing? Maybe it's better that it happened this way. There was no pain. No suffering."

Maybe not for Margaret. But for her family?

"Not just her passing. I just need time to think. About everything."

"Okay. I get that."

But she didn't. He could tell.

"Call me if you need anything, okay?"

Her hand fell back to her side. "I will." She paused for a second. "Does some of what you need to think about revolve around what happened last night?"

"We can talk about it later."

"So it does."

He swallowed. He didn't want to hurt her, but wasn't that inevitable at this point? The thought of being involved with someone caused a queasiness to churn inside of him that no amount of talking would abolish. It was a knee-jerk reaction that made no sense, and yet, try as he might, he'd never been able to rid himself of it. He was like Walter Grapevine, forever stuck on a dead-end path, but not able—no… not *willing*—to change.

He moved forward and took her hand. "Evie, last night was a mistake."

"A mistake. Why?"

"I can't explain it. But I don't have what it takes to truly give myself over to someone else. Maybe it's from my childhood. Maybe it's engraved into my DNA. I don't know. But I only know I'm not what you need."

She jerked her hand free, her eyebrows going up. "I think *I* should be the one to decide that. But since every single time we start to move toward something deeper, you stop and call it a mistake… Well, this time, I'll believe you. So let's just say it's over and move on."

Hearing her cast the very words he'd been thinking into the universe was a shock. And for a second, he wondered if he'd done the right thing. But right or not, it was too late now.

As if emphasizing her point, she went over to the table, snatched up the condom and walked back over to him. She put it in his hand and curled his fingers around it. "Take it. You'll need it for the next woman you decide to have sex with. Only let me give you a piece of advice. Don't tell her it was a mistake."

Before he could say anything else, she

walked past him to the bathroom and went inside, softly closing the door behind her.

He should be glad. Evie had let him off easy. But something about the way she'd said that he'd need that condom for the next woman sent a knife deep into his chest. Is that what she thought he did?

Don't you? Didn't you just think about how you don't have sex with women you care about?

He stared at the object in his hand, horrified at the truth that was staring him right in the face. And then he went over and dropped it into the garbage can by the bed. He finished dressing and left Evie's apartment, getting into his car and driving with no destination in mind. The only thing he wanted to do was escape. Escape the news of Margaret's death. Escape the fact that what had happened with Evie was done for good. And that there was no going back.

"In short, it was a mistake. According to Max."

She'd met Darby at her office shortly after he'd left her apartment. She couldn't believe how easy it had seemed for him to throw words at her that hurt her to the core.

"Maybe give him some time. I always felt

like there was something he wanted to tell you, but just never could."

"I think he pretty much said everything he wanted to say. And when I told him it was over and we should move on, he didn't say a word."

"Do you love him, Evie?"

Those words shocked her into silence for several minutes. Then, in complete misery, she nodded. "I do. I think I have for a very long time. I was just too afraid to admit it to myself." She let out a hard laugh. "And it looks like I was right in being afraid. Thank God, I didn't say it this morning or last night. Because I'm pretty sure he would have thrown it back in my face."

"You don't know that."

"I do. You didn't see the look he gave me when I asked him to stop and talk to me. He acted like I was made of poison."

"I'm so sorry, Evie. Do you want me to talk to him?"

The thought of that filled her with horror. "No. Please don't say anything to him. I don't even want him to know that you know."

"There's no way he won't. He knows how close we are."

She thought for a minute. "You're right. Because here I am less than two hours after he left my apartment. And I don't really need advice. I just needed to tell someone. Losing Margaret and Max in one day…"

Darby put her cane against her desk and caught her up in a tight hug. "I'm sorry, honey. So, so sorry. I thought… Well, never mind what I thought, because that doesn't matter. And I know you don't want advice, so all I'm going to say is that you need to give yourselves space and time to heal. Maybe you'll both either realize that what happened isn't the end of the world. Or you'll realize it is and that you can't live without each other."

"I don't see that second option ever happening, but I do think you're right about the first one. And since Margaret was the only patient we had in common right now, there shouldn't be a lot of reasons to see each other."

"What about the gala?"

"That planning is all done. No need for any more meetings, and as for the event itself, there should be enough people there that we can avoid crossing paths during it." She shrugged. "I've never thought about leaving Nevada, but maybe I need to go visit some of my relatives in Brazil for a couple of weeks. I have a lot of vacation time saved up. I can be back in time to make sure all of the gala stuff is ready to go."

"I think that's a good idea. I'll miss you. And please don't leave Nevada. Not permanently. Not without giving yourself a lot of time to think and grieve. And this is worth grieving over, Evie. You love him. Let yourself cry and scream and shake your fist at the sky. But don't make a permanent decision while you're feeling like this."

"I won't. I have a few patients I need to wrap up over the next week and then I'll spend a week or two in Brazil. Once the gala is over, I think I'll be able to screw my head back on straight and figure out my next step."

She wanted to make sure that Delilah, especially, was doing okay before she left. She had a track meet today, so Evie would call this afternoon and find out how it went. And then she had another two patients who were in the middle of adjusting meds and she wanted to see those through as well. And then she'd be free to go to Brazil and try to clear her mind of anything that had to do with Max or what had happened between them. And he was right. This could never happen again, because it would destroy her. So even if she had to walk away from him, from his friendship, she was going to do what she needed to keep from being hurt by him ever again.

* * *

Max twirled a pencil between his fingers, then tossed it to the top of the desk and groaned out loud. He'd gone to Margaret's memorial service two days ago and had seen Evie from afar. He'd toyed with going over to her afterward to see how she was doing, but she must have slipped out as soon as it ended. When he looked for her, there was no sign of her.

He hadn't seen her in the hospital, either, but that wasn't all that unusual. Unless their paths happened to cross because one of their patients needed services that the other specialized in, they pretty much kept to their own departments. But he hadn't even caught sight of her since the service. And he couldn't stop thinking about her. About how they'd left things.

No. Not *they*. Him. Max was the one who'd had the meltdown and had said a lot of things he didn't mean. A lot of things he regretted. And a week after Margaret's death he could see that he'd mentally blamed Evie for getting through to his heart, when all along it had been Max who'd opened the door and let her in.

Blaming her was probably just an excuse to run for the door. What he really hadn't been able to face wasn't Margaret's death—it was what had happened in Evie's bedroom.

But why had he made it into such a tragedy? Why had he felt like the world was ending, when it really was still spinning on its axis just like it always had?

Everything inside of him went silent for several seconds. All thought ceased. His muscles froze, breathing stopped, then it all started back up again when the truth he'd been avoiding exploded onto the scene, scorching everything he thought he knew.

He loved her.

And that was why he'd been so horrified. And so adamant that it had meant nothing, and tried to convince not just himself, but her.

All because of the baggage he carried from his mom and his dad. And it wasn't even their fault. It was his for taking on their problems and acting like they were going to be repeated in his life. They weren't. Max hadn't gone out and drunk himself into a stupor when Evie had let him walk out of her life. Evie wasn't the one who'd died, it was one of their patients. And while that fact made him sad and he had grieved the things that she would never get to do, he was going to be able to move past it and keep on living.

What he wasn't sure of was whether he was going to be able to move past Evie. And he suddenly knew he didn't want to. He wanted to hold her in his arms and say he was sorry for every stupid thing he'd ever said to her. Sleeping with her hadn't been a mistake. It had been the smartest thing he'd ever done. Because it had made him stop and take a good look at what was staring him in the face. What had been staring him in the face since before she'd met Brad. That he loved her. It was why Brad and Dale's interest in her had bothered him so much. Why he hadn't been able to stand the sight of her with another man.

So what was he going to do? He was going to find her and do what he'd just thought about. He was going to take her in his arms and tell her how much he loved her. And beg for her forgiveness for wasting so many years of their lives.

He took a deep breath and picked up the pencil, then tossed it in the air and caught it by its point. But he couldn't do any of that sitting here at his desk. He wasn't sure she could forgive him, or if she even should, but what he was sure of was that he needed to try. Right now. After telling his assistant where she could find him, he headed down the elevator to her department and went to the desk. "Is Dr. Milagre here?"

"No. She actually left for vacation this morning."

A cold wind washed over him. Was that a euphemism for leaving? For good?

"Do you know when she'll be back?"

The woman glanced at a calendar in front of her. "She said if things went well she'd be back…let's see. Yes, here it is. A week before the gala. July twenty-fifth."

If things went well. And if they didn't? "Okay, thanks."

He left and did the only thing he could think of. He called Darby.

"Nao sei."

God, how many times was Evie going to have to explain to her well-meaning relatives that she didn't know if she was ever going to get married again. Or if she was going to have children before she was forty years old.

She thought coming here had been a good idea, but a week in, it looked like it might have been the worst idea of her life. She missed her job, missed her apartment, but most of all she missed Max. Despite what they'd said to each other, she regretted leaving without getting some kind of closure, even if it meant the end of their friendship. She regretted not having her say and not telling him the truth once she'd realized it: that she loved him. Confessing it didn't demand that he feel the same way, it was simply telling him the truth. How much worse could it be than leaving things the way they had?

Her aunt was saying something and she'd missed it.

"Como?"

"I asked if you'd mind riding with me to the airport to meet a friend. I hate driving in that traffic alone."

"Why don't you take the bus?" The bus that went from São Paulo to the international airport was a lot easier than driving. And it only took about forty minutes.

"It's a special friend, and I want him to be comfortable."

Evie's eyebrows shot up. "Aunt Maria, do you have a *namorado*?" Her aunt had never been married and she was pushing seventy.

"Of course not, *moça*. Grab your purse, we need to go."

Okay, so it had gone from asking Evie if she wanted to go to assuming that she would. But what else did she have to do? She still had two more days before her own flight for the States, and the way she felt right now, it could not arrive fast enough. "Okay, I'll be right back."

Then they were in the car and driving through the snarls of rush-hour traffic, but her aunt, to her credit, was very good at weaving in and out of traffic at just the right moment to keep inching forward. If you made eye contact with the next driver, it was an unspoken rule that they had to let you in. And Aunt Maria was a force of nature when it came to getting people to look at her.

Once they were at the airport, Maria checked the flights while Evie moped in silence. "I found it, let's go."

Her aunt pulled her behind her until they were at the arrivals area. Evie hoped whoever it was got here quickly. All she wanted to do was get back to the house so she could start packing for her return flight. Darby had kept her apprised of how the gala preparations were going—since she and Max were still on speaking terms. The workmen had almost completed the courtyard and the obelisk structure had been carted away to parts unknown.

"There. He is here."

She glanced up, only half interested in whoever it was. She'd been gone from Brazil for so many years that it was doubtful that she even knew the person. "Where?"

"Just look. You will see him."

Oh, brother. She looked at the throng of people, not seeing a single familiar face. Then her attention snagged on something. An easy move of masculine hips that looked familiar. She frowned and looked closer at the people coming toward them. Then she blinked, every emotion in her suddenly rushing up and getting stuck in her throat.

It couldn't be.

She lost sight of him for a second, then as she frantically swept her gaze across the group, he reappeared behind someone. Oh, God, it was.

Max!

She jerked around to look at her aunt, who only nodded. "Yes, *querida*, it is him."

"But how?"

"Your friend Darby called your mother, who called us and told us he was flying into Brazil. It is why I insisted you come."

Was he here for a conference and her mom had somehow found out? The shot of happiness she'd felt vanished. What if he wasn't here for *her* at all?

Then their eyes met and he stopped, right in the middle of the moving line of people, forcing the crowd to part and go around him like water flowing around a rock.

Then he was moving again, his lanky frame eating up the distance before she had a chance to catch her breath. Then she was in his arms and he held her so tightly that she really *couldn't* breathe.

Was this happening? Maybe this was all some dream or wishful thinking. Maybe her longing was so strong that she'd summoned a hallucination. And yet, his arms felt real. And he was murmuring something in her ear over and over.

It was her name.

And for some reason it broke her, and she started sobbing, clinging to him like he was the only thing that could save her world. And maybe he wasn't, but he was the closest thing she was going to find.

He pulled back, looking into her face. A thumb came up and captured a drop of moisture. "Happy tears or sad?"

She sucked down a shuddering breath. "That depends on why you're here."

"I'm here for you."

Her eyes closed and she pulled his face down to her, pressing her cheek against his. "Happy. They're happy tears. I love you, Max."

He kissed her, the softest touch, almost making her cry again. She thought she knew what it meant, but she wanted to hear the words. Needed to hear them. He looked at her and nodded. "I love you, too. I was just too afraid to admit it. Or to believe I deserved it. And so I ran. And worse, I called something beautiful a mistake, hoping it would make you pull away. And it did. But it was the stupidest thing I've ever said and it wasn't true. It wasn't a mistake. You'll always be my best friend, Evie. But I'd like the chance for it to be more than that."

"Yes."

He laughed, pulling back and putting an arm around her waist. "Yes, what?"

"Yes to whatever you suggest, as long as it includes having you in my life."

"That's a nonnegotiable." He glanced to the side and saw an older lady who looked far too pleased to not be a part of how he'd gotten to Brazil. "Is this your aunt?"

"Oh, yes." She turned red. "I'm sorry. Aunt Maria, this is Max, my…"

"Teu namorado. Ja sei." The woman stepped forward and kissed him on either cheek. *"Bem vindo ao Brasil."*

Max's head tilted, and Evie laughed. "I'll explain what she said later. But right now, all

I want to do is this." She went up on tiptoe and kissed him again. "I just want to hold your hand all the way to my aunt's house. And then I still want to be holding it in two days, as we head home."

"Home," he said. "I like the sound of that." With that, he gripped her hand and followed her aunt to the airport's exit, where they stepped out into brilliant sunshine and the promise of a thousand more days just like this one.

Just then her phone pinged, and she glanced at the readout. "Oh, my God," she whispered.

"What is it?" Max sounded worried.

"It's Darby. She said it's raining in Las Vegas and more is predicted over the next couple of days. The drought is over."

"It certainly is." Only Max wasn't looking at her phone. He was looking at her. And in his expression was more love than she ever dreamed possible.

She squeezed his hand in silent agreement. The drought was over. And she thanked God for the rain.

EPILOGUE

Two years later

MAX CAUGHT SIGHT of Evie coming toward him across the courtyard. It was their second gala as husband and wife and he would never get tired of the sight of her in an evening gown. Even eight months pregnant, she was the most beautiful woman in the room. And she was all his.

At thirty-eight, she was considered a high-risk pregnancy and Max had to fight the urge to coddle her and make her slow down. But Evie swore she would not do anything that would put their baby at risk. Her mom and dad and whole extended family were ecstatic with the fact that their family was about to grow. And Max had been welcomed in as if he'd always belonged, and he loved it. Loved them all. He was even trying to learn Portuguese, although Evie always translated for him.

He tucked her arm through his and dropped a kiss on her head. "Have I told you I loved you lately?"

"Hmm." She hummed the sound in that low throaty way of hers that drove him crazy. "Only about forty times."

"Then I'm behind schedule." He nodded toward the left. "Come dance with me."

"Now? I'm not sure I'll make the best partner." She cupped her belly.

He tipped up her chin and looked into her eyes. "You make the best partner all the time. Please. For me."

"Okay." They walked over to the area where the dance floor had been set up. The same dance floor that had been used for the last two years, since the hospital portion of the gala had been everyone's favorite part. And Evie was still head of that committee. Morgan Howard's successor had finally been chosen and it was actually his son, who was also a doctor. And Morgan Howard the second was every bit as compassionate and savvy as his father was. Everyone loved him.

DJ Electric Nights saw them coming and winked at him. "All set?"

"Yes, we're all set."

Evie looked up at him in question and the

music started softly, then slowly got louder. She bit her lip. "Max, you know this song always makes me cry."

"That's why I wanted him to play it." He took her in his arms and slowly moved in time with the music, the country singer's voice coming through with a sure sincerity that said he knew what he was singing about.

Evie laid her head against his chest and closed her eyes as they swayed together. No one else in the world mattered, except the woman in his arms. The first verse moved into the chorus and then flowed to the second stanza. Through each word and phrase, Max took them in and made them into a vow he would never go back on. She was the best thing that had ever happened to him.

The chorus came for the last time and the singer seemed to hang on to those final words for a long time. Long enough for Max to sing them softly in her ear. "You're my best friend... my best friend."

* * * * *

If you enjoyed this story,
check out these other great reads from
Tina Beckett

Reunion with the ER Doctor
ER Doc's Miracle Triplets
Tempting the Off-Limits Nurse
A Daddy for the Midwife's Twins?

All available now!

HARLEQUIN
Reader Service

Enjoyed your book?

Try the perfect subscription for Romance readers and get more great books like this delivered right to your door.

See why over 10+ million readers have tried Harlequin Reader Service.

Start with a Free Welcome Collection with free books and a gift—valued over $20.

Choose any series in print or ebook. See website for details and order today:

   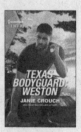

TryReaderService.com/subscriptions